The Sacrifice

Even the book morphs!
Flip the pages
and check it out!

Look for other ANIMORPHS®
titles by K.A. Applegate:

#1 The Invasion
#2 The Visitor
#3 The Encounter
#4 The Message
#5 The Predator
#6 The Capture
#7 The Stranger
#8 The Alien
#9 The Secret
#10 The Android
#11 The Forgotten
#12 The Reaction
#13 The Change
#14 The Unknown
#15 The Escape
#16 The Warning
#17 The Underground
#18 The Decision
#19 The Departure
#20 The Discovery
#21 The Threat
#22 The Solution
#23 The Pretender
#24 The Suspicion
#25 The Extreme
#26 The Attack
#27 The Exposed
#28 The Experiment
#29 The Sickness
#30 The Reunion
#31 The Conspiracy
#32 The Separation
#33 The Illusion
#34 The Prophecy
#35 The Proposal
#36 The Mutation
#37 The Weakness
#38 The Arrival
#39 The Hidden
#40 The Other
#41 The Familiar
#42 The Journey
#43 The Test
#44 The Unexpected
#45 The Revelation
#46 The Deception
#47 The Resistance
#48 The Return
#49 The Diversion
#50 The Ultimate
#51 The Absolute

<MEGAMORPHS>

#1 The Andalite's Gift
#2 In the Time of Dinosaurs
#3 Elfangor's Secret
#4 Back to Before

The Andalite Chronicles

The Hork-Bajir Chronicles
Visser
The Ellimist Chronicles

ALTERNAMORPHS

The First Journey
The Next Passage

ANIMORPHS®

The Sacrifice

K.A. Applegate

AN
APPLE
PAPERBACK

SCHOLASTIC INC.
New York Toronto London Auckland Sydney
Mexico City New Delhi Hong Kong

Cover illustration by David B. Mattingly
Art Direction/Design by Karen Hudson/Ursula Albano

ISBN 0-439-11526-4

12 11 10 9 8 7 6 5 4 3 2 1 1 2 3 4 5 6/0

Printed in the U.S.A.
First Scholastic printing, April 2001

The author wishes to thank Kim Morris for her help in preparing this manuscript.

And for Michael and Jake

The Sacrifice

Even the book morphs!
Flip the pages
and check it out!

CHAPTER 1

<Heads up. Something's definitely going down.> Rachel, in bald eagle morph, braked and swooped and circled.

James, in peregrine falcon morph, followed, circling almost in tandem with Rachel.

That kind of close formation flying was a mistake.

Different species of birds of prey do not typically fly together, especially in synchronized motion.

I was in northern harrier morph, several feet above my companions and hanging back. Trying to keep a reasonable distance between us in case we were being observed from the ground.

I wondered if Rachel would rebuke James. He was new and sometimes made minor mistakes.

But Rachel was too eager to pursue her investigation into what was taking place on the ground below to correct James.

I, too, said nothing to James. Of all the Animorphs, I had been most opposed to our recruiting handicapped young humans to be warriors alongside us in our fight against the Yeerks. So far, the overall performance of James and the others had set my mind somewhat at ease.

Still, I was uncomfortable treating James and his team as a true part of the resistance.

And even after all this time on my adopted planet, Earth, I was acutely aware of being an outsider. The only Andalite, the only alien in our band of guerrillas. Though on several occasions I had spoken my mind, on many others I had hesitated to do so.

I had no real authority over James or Rachel. They were likely to reject any instructions or directives from me.

Rachel, because she listened to no one but Jake, and then, often with barely concealed resentment. And James, because he acted as leader and to some degree protector, of the seventeen new recruits. James was Jake's lieutenant.

Jake is our leader. He had sent the three of us

on a reconnaissance mission. We were to make note of what was happening in the city and report back to our base of operations. The secret Hork-Bajir camp.

I doubt that Jake had anticipated anything as dramatic as what I saw below me. It appeared that the city was under military occupation.

Police, uniformed military men and women, and official trucks and cars blocked off many streets.

Drivers were being stopped and asked to exit their cars. Then they were taken to join the crowds of people being diverted into train stations at gunpoint.

<What's going on?> James asked. <Are those people being protected, or persecuted? Evacuated for their own protection? Or being taken prisoner?>

<I can't tell,> Rachel answered. <That's the problem when the good guys and the bad guys all look alike. It's hard to know who's an uninfested human and who's a Controller. This war gets more complicated every day.>

I agreed with Rachel's statement.

My name is Aximili-Esgarrouth-Isthill. It is my real name. The others do not use their real names, though at this point, they could do so without increasing the danger of discovery.

Our identities are known now to our enemies. We have been exposed. The danger could not get any nearer, clearer, or greater.

Furthermore, our best weapon, the blue box, has fallen into the hands of the enemy. They now have the same Andalite morphing technology as we do.

It has always been difficult to distinguish humans from human-Controllers. At least at a glance. Now it is also difficult to distinguish real animals from morphed human-Controllers.

I don't think I'm doing a very good job of explaining our situation.

Jake is very good at explaining.

I will try again.

A race of aliens that resemble large slugs has invaded Earth. The aliens are called Yeerks.

Since the Yeerks have no useful bodies of their own — no means of movement, virtually no sensory abilities — they search out host bodies. They are parasites.

The human and the Yeerk coexist. But the relationship is far from symbiotic. The Yeerk is in total control.

The Yeerks' plan is to use Earth as a hub planet. Here they can potentially acquire millions of host bodies. A massive force of human-Controllers will enable them to effectively push out into other galaxies.

The Yeerks have already enslaved other species to use as hosts. For example, the Hork-Bajir and the Taxxons.

Hork-Bajir have excellent bodies for purposes of combat. They are seven feet tall with blades on their elbows and knees, foreheads and wrists. They somewhat resemble the long extinct reptilian creatures humans call dinosaurs.

Taxxon bodies are large and unwieldy, like a massive sack of guts. They possess hundreds of centipedelike arms and legs. Their mouths are rimmed with razor-sharp teeth. Their eyes are red and gelatinous.

Because of their voracious hunger, Taxxons are excellent at instilling terror. Once they sense blood, they cannot be turned back, even if it means their own deaths. They are driven by a ravenous hunger that never, ever abates.

It is difficult sometimes not to pity them.

Of course, the bodies the Yeerks covet the most are bodies like mine. Andalite bodies.

Andalites have four legs. This gives us the speed of horses. We have two pairs of eyes, one pair on stalks. This enables us to see in all directions at once.

We have the ability to speak without using our mouths. This is very fortunate considering Andalites have no mouths.

For purposes of combat, our tails are equipped with a deadly sharp blade.

But it is our ability to morph, to transform into other creatures, that makes our species the envy of the galaxy.

Only one Yeerk has ever succeeded in acquiring an Andalite body. Visser One. The leader of the Yeerk invasion.

For that desecration of my species, I hate him.

And for killing my brother, Elfangor.

CHAPTER 2

<Okay. No doubt about what's going on,> Rachel said angrily. <I see a pair of Hork-Bajir directing people into a subway station. And the people don't want to go. This is a Yeerk operation.>

<Oh, yeah. That roundup is definitely not for the citizens' protection,> James said.

James was new. He was still learning. But he was smart and learning fast.

<Human-Controllers, too,> Rachel noted. <Guns and Dracons.>

James circled, maintaining his altitude. <Question is, why are the Yeerks herding people into a subway station?>

<Trains are a good way of transporting a lot of people at the same time. And fast,> Rachel replied grimly.

<The Yeerk pool,> I said. <I would assume that is their destination.>

<Where Yeerks live when they don't have a host body.> James. <Where they feed, too, right? If the Yeerks are taking humans to the pool in big groups, it means they're mass-producing new human-Controllers.>

<A Contoller factory. Assembly line and all. It's sick.>

Rachel and James were discussing the Yeerk pools. It's a pretty basic concept. Yeerks must feed every three days. The majority of Controllers, not important enough to be in possession of private, portable pools, must journey to a central place to absorb the life-sustaining Kandrona rays.

If the Yeerk is deprived of Kandrona rays, a painful process of starvation ensues.

<The Yeerk pool is only a train ride away,> James said wryly. <Very convenient. The Yeerks have solved the problem of commuting. Provide your employees with free transportation.>

<Feeding a large number of Controllers is the one difficulty the Yeerks have not yet successfully mastered,> I said thoughtfully. <The Yeerk

pool has always been the one sure place we have been able to cause serious disruption.>

We, the resistance, the Animorphs, have located, damaged, or destroyed more than one Yeerk pool and Kandrona source.

Animorphs. Marco coined the term back before I was rescued and joined the team. The original members of the Animorphs are Jake, Rachel, Cassie, Tobias, Marco. And me. The only Andalite.

None of us are adults. The others are now of the age to be attending what humans call "high school."

We have no "high school" on the Andalite home planet. But we do have the Academy. I was an *aristh* in the Academy. What humans would call a "cadet."

My brother, Elfangor, was a great Andalite military hero. He was killed here on Earth by Visser One, then known as Visser Three, leader of the Yeerk invasion.

Before he died, Elfangor gave the morphing cube to this group of human young people. The ones who call themselves the Animorphs.

For a long time, we were the only ones with the ability to morph. Us and, of course, Visser One, who only had the ability because his host body was an Andalite.

In our last major battle, the Yeerks were able to steal the blue morphing cube that transfers the morphing technology. Thus, we have lost our one true advantage.

But while we still had the cube, Jake realized that in order to continue the fight against the Yeerks we needed to increase our ranks. As I mentioned, I was wary of the decision to enlist handicapped children, mostly due to their lack of combat experience.

However, I could not deny that because the Yeerks would never consider handicapped human bodies suitable hosts, these children were likely to be uninfested.

There are seventeen new recruits, including James, the boy called Tuan, and the girls called Kelly and Collette.

On my planet we call such individuals *vecols.* Andalite custom ordains these disabled live in isolation. It is largely for their own sake, as they would feel great shame as part of society. So it is out of respect for *vecols* that they are kept from full participation in the world.

My experiences on Earth, however, have led me to question the wisdom of the Andalite custom. Not that human custom regarding the disabled or handicapped is not also flawed.

As we suspected, a few of the new recruits were healed by the morphing process. Only three, James and Craig and Erica. Their healthy DNA was restored although they have sworn to continue life as handicapped people. For security reasons. At least until the war is over.

James is a good soldier. They all are. But inexperienced.

I felt we should proceed no further on our own. <We should report this to Jake immediately,> I said.

<No time,> Rachel replied tersely. <Ax, look at all those people being forced into the subway! In just a few hours, the Yeerks could produce another thousand human-Controllers.>

<So, what do we do?> James asked.

I could hear the eagerness in his voice. The eagerness of a new soldier. One not yet exhausted and sickened by war.

<Let's see if we can either close that tunnel down or slow up production,> Rachel answered.

It was a foolish course of action. There were only three of us. Yes, we had been clever and productive in the past. But that was before the Yeerks had forced us to become refugees.

<Ax?> Rachel prompted. <Are you in or are you out?>

<I think we should talk to Jake,> I repeated.

<Look, those are innocent people down there.> James's voice was getting angry. <Don't you care?>

Innocent people.

Humans.

Did James mean that he did not consider me part of their team because I am not human?

I am not an adult, but I am not a child, either. My feelings are not easily hurt.

But still, I could not help but think it odd that James would seem to feel the need to instruct me as to what emotions were appropriate in this situation. And to question my loyalty.

I was still trying to decide what to say, when we heard the bloodcurdling cry.

Something swooped past me, clipped my wings, and sent me spinning.

I heard cries of surprise from James and Rachel, too.

I righted myself in the air. Felt talons rake my back! I shot forward, out of my attacker's clutches. I poured on a burst of speed and wheeled to see what had attacked.

A group of peregrine falcons, reforming to strike again. Yeerks in morph.

I saw James bleeding and circling downward with a broken wing.

Rachel flew, talons extended, beak open, rushing the falcons.

The Yeerk-falcons scattered with cries of alarm and then divided into two groups of three.

One group headed for me.

The other group headed for Rachel.

It was interesting that none of them pursued James. They must have thought he was a real falcon. Or maybe they thought he was already dead.

<Still want to report back?> Rachel asked.

<I do not think it is an option now,> I replied.

CHAPTER 3

Rachel and I streaked down toward the crowd of people being hustled into the subway station.

Several of the uninfested humans saw us and screamed. Others ducked and covered their heads with their arms.

We must have been an odd and frightening sight. A screeching eagle. A northern harrier. And six peregrine falcons giving chase.

Tseew! Tseew!

Dracon fire! But the beams went wide and hit the concrete overhang of the subway station. Shattered the tile sign that announced the station's name.

The Dracon fire created a panic. The crowd

surged back, away from the subway station entrance. Several people were being trampled.

But the Hork-Bajir guards ignored the injured humans. They quickly formed a barricade behind the crowd and continued to herd their prisoners down the station's stairs.

<Here we go!>

Whoosh!

Rachel tucked her massive wings back against her body and zoomed down into the subway station. I followed into the relative dark. My feathers skimmed the heads of the taller humans. And every instinct of the bird and the Andalite recoiled at entering a confined and relatively airless space headfirst.

Near the bottom of the stairs, first Rachel, then I thrust our feet and swept our wings forward to help slow us down. When we reached the platform we righted ourselves, flapped hard to maintain stable, even flight.

Rachel and I were inside the tunnel now.

And we could hear the cries of the pursuing falcons.

<Ax, Rachel? Can you guys hear me? If you can, I demorphed, remorphed, and followed you in. I'm on your tails, behind these Yeerk jerks. And they're even worse at flying in this place than I am.>

The fact is that peregrine falcons are incredi-

bly fast flyers. But the Yeerks' inexperience with their morphs and their own arrogant characters would work to our advantage now. At least I hoped so.

Beneath us, humans continued to stream down onto the subway platform.

A train sped by. The noise was disconcerting to both my Andalite brain and the harrier brain. Through the dirty windows of the train cars I saw far too many scared human faces.

This train was obviously Yeerk-controlled. And there was no choice but to follow it into the ever-darkening tunnel. The falcons would be on us in moments.

Through the tunnel we flew. We tried to fly above the rushing train, not directly behind it.

<What a ride!> Rachel screamed.

I agreed. Even flying above the train we were pulled along by its draft. Exciting, in one way. Terrifying in another.

But it was no use. Even with this advantage, the six Yeerk-infested falcons were closing in. Their desire to reach us was clearly overriding their inexperience and the difficulties of underground flight.

<Land on the roof of the train!> I called. <We'll let the train lose them for us!>

Imagine it.

The train whizzed beneath us but always

pulling ahead. At my estimation it was traveling at approximately forty to forty-five miles per hour, creating the interesting optical illusion that there was no separation between cars. And that we were no longer moving at all.

In short, the train was traveling far, far faster than any of us could fly.

To land would be incredibly dangerous. But it was the only way we could possibly outfly the Yeerks.

I kept my eyes focused for something, anything, to grip and hold on to. After a moment or two my eyes adjusted to the darkness. I could make out individual components of what had been just a long, blurred strip of metal. Now I saw that along the right and left side of each car's roof was a raised lip. <Rachel. There. On the left and right edge. A ridge.>

<I see it,> Rachel responded. <James? You still with the Yeerks?>

<Right behind you.>

<Okay, Ax. Go!>

CHAPTER 4

The train roared beneath me. I swept my wings forward to kill air speed. It didn't slow me down much. The drag was too great.

I hit the top of the train hard. But my talons managed to catch the lip. Barely. I kept my wings forward and the rest of me strained back to slow my body's momentum. If I pitched forward and fell, I would have great difficulty righting myself without letting go of the lip. And without flying off the train and shooting headfirst into the wall of the tunnel.

The effort was great but it was not the first time I had landed on a moving vehicle. I managed to stay upright by hunkering down as close to the roof as I could.

A moment later, Rachel landed on the car behind me. <I SO love doing that,> she laughed.

<I'm on,> James called a moment after that. <And I do NOT love doing that.>

Further along the dark tunnel we raced. Carefully, without letting go and using my wings for balance, I glanced behind me.

We seemed to have lost our pursuers. It was time to abandon the train before it brought us into the Yeerk pool complex unprepared.

It was definitely time to morph.

One by one we opened our wings to catch the current and . . .

WHOOOSH!

Were torn off the roof of the train, tossed backward like tumbleweeds in a tornado, tumbling, whirling, spinning!

<Woo hoo!> Rachel, of course.

One by one we fought to get control of our bodies, land without serious injury on the tunnel's narrow walkway.

<This falcon is nauseous,> James said. <Is that possible? Please tell me I'm not going to hurl.>

<I personally have never known a falcon to throw up,> I said. <But you might want to demorph just in case.>

<Yeah,> Rachel said. <And then morph something big and mean. Something that will help us fight our way out.>

As we've mentioned in the past, morphing isn't graceful or pretty. And it is quite unpredictable.

SPLOOOT. SPLOOOT.

Fortunately, my legs were the first part of my Andalite body to emerge. I felt a strange tingling as my tail began to sprout from the harrier's tail feathers.

<There they are!> The Yeerk-falcons were back.

And none of us was entirely finished with our morphs.

But my Andalite tail was now fully emerged.

The blade was in place. Along with one stalk eye bursting from my still-feathered head.

<Don't let them get away!!> The angry voice of a Yeerk-falcon.

<I'll take the Andalite!> another shouted.

I saw the falcon hurtle toward me in the dark. I lifted my tail, and WHAP! Sent him flying like a tennis ball.

THUMP!

Five Yeerk-falcons left.

Peregrine falcons in a pack might be a danger to a lone northern harrier, but they are a minor nuisance to an Andalite. A second falcon screamed and zoomed in toward me. I lifted my tail and the bird was no longer a problem.

Hurriedly I completed the morph. Rachel was behind me. She had reversed her morph and was in her eagle morph again. But a bald eagle on the ground is not as deadly as one in the air. And it would be difficult for her to lift off in the stifling tunnel.

James, the least experienced of us, had not begun his remorph. He crouched against the tunnel's grimy wall, reluctant to let the Yeerks identify a new human resistor. One who was supposed to be paralyzed and in a wheelchair.

It was up to me. Only four Yeerk-falcons remained but they were angry.

That's when I saw it.

A low-hanging electrical conduit. Live.

<Rachel, James,> I said in private thought-speak. <I am going to cut the lights. Be prepared.>

<Go for it, Ax-man.>

I lifted my tail and aimed. Fortunately, the blade on my tail is not metal and my hooves would ground me. I felt nothing but a slight flutter through my body as my tail blade sliced through the electrical conduit that powered the tunnel's lighting system.

The dim lights in the tunnel went dark.

I waited the few seconds it would take my eyes to adjust to the gloom. When they did, I still could see no more than dark and darker shapes.

<Whoa,> James whispered. <I'm almost all lion now. The lion's eyes are seeing more than the falcons' in this light.>

The unexpected turn of events had momentarily confused the Yeerk-falcons. I heard low muttering from them but no screams of attack.

And Rachel had begun to morph again.

CHAPTER 5

It took her only moments. And then she was a great horned owl.

The four remaining falcons had re-formed and were coming at me. Even in the darkness they would provide relatively easy targets.

I lifted my tail blade in preparation.

When they were only two feet away . . .

WHOOOOSH!

I did not hear Rachel fly past me. I felt Rachel fly past me.

Owl feathers are the softest feathers imaginable. The result is that owls can fly making no sound at all.

The falcons never even heard her coming.

Rachel took down the first falcon with her

talons neatly and dropping it to the tracks below. The remaining three falcons wheeled away.

Rachel followed them. <It's not so easy, is it, Yeerks?> she taunted. <You don't just turn into animals and everything is fine. It's harder than it looks, isn't it?>

The falcons crowded at a turn in the tunnel. One of them collided into a wall. He let out a cry of alarm and fell to the ground.

The Yeerk-falcons were disoriented. Confused and panicking.

I watched as the fallen falcon demorphed and then began to morph to Hork-Bajir.

Before he could complete the morph, there was a terrifying scream and a lion leaped out of the dark. James.

I heard the Yeerk's last words. <No! No! Don't want to . . . die . . . please . . . aaagh . . .>

I did not like it. I am a soldier. But there was something unseemly about dying in a dark and filthy tunnel in midmorph.

I heard a sound that was even worse. Cries of victory and satisfaction from Rachel as she downed another of the falcons.

The other Animorphs and I truly worry about Rachel.

On the Andalite home planet, when a warrior becomes too fond of war he is shunned. A warrior should love only the cause not the killing.

If Rachel were an Andalite . . .

But, she is not. And I am not a human.

Only one Yeerk-falcon remained. Perhaps it had escaped Rachel.

But we had bigger problems now. Out of the dark three Hork-Bajir came trotting toward us like commandos with a very serious purpose.

The lights had been cut. Members of the resistance had been spotted entering the subway station. They were coming to investigate. But in the near-total blackness the Hork-Bajir could not see me or James directly in their path. They could not hear Rachel coming up from behind.

We were ready.

Rachel buzzed the guards. One of the Hork-Bajir reeled back and fell onto the train tracks. On the way his elbow blades accidentally sliced into the stomach of the second Hork-Bajir. There was a horrible moaning as both were electrocuted by the live third rail.

James took care of the third Hork-Bajir.

And then with one stalk eye I spotted the remaining Yeerk-falcon streaking toward me. It was a bold and brave move but he was the enemy.

I lifted my tail and struck with the flat of my blade. The blow brought him down but did not kill him.

I bent quickly and picked him up.

<Let me go!> he begged. <Please let me go. I am so close. Only minutes away.>

<Minutes away from what?> I asked.

<It only takes two hours. Right? I've been a falcon for one hour and fifty-five minutes. In five minutes I'll be free!>

So. This creature wanted to be a *nothlit.* Wanted to be trapped in his morph.

<You will not be free. You will still be a Yeerk inside,> I pointed out.

<I will be free,> the falcon insisted. <I will fly. I will see. No more need for Kandrona. No more orders, no more of this horrible war. I'll just fly away.>

I understood. This creature was like Tobias, my true *shorm.* What a human would call my "best friend."

Tobias was once a human boy. A very unhappy human boy. He stayed in red-tailed hawk morph for longer than two hours. I suspect he did it on purpose. It was his way of escaping the complexities of human life. Although he exchanged them for a new set of complexities.

It was logical that among the Yeerks there might also be those who felt overwhelmed by the demands of war. I knew of the Yeerk resistance. With Cassie's encouragement we had allowed one of its freedom fighters to morph a humpback whale and escape life as a parasite. In exchange for this gift, Aftran had promised never to reveal our identities to the Yeerks.

I said nothing but I released him. Gently I tossed him into the air.

<Thank you!> he cried gratefully. I watched as the falcon flew off down the tunnel and disappeared into the dark.

I did not notice Rachel zooming after him.

CHAPTER 6

<Aaaaaahhhh!>

Suddenly, there was an eruption of screams and screeches from down the tunnel. A human voice. The cries of a peregrine falcon.

Rachel.

Had she caught the Yeerk-falcon?

I did not know.

I did not want to know.

But our ill-conceived, spur-of-the-moment mission had not succeeded. Had any of us really thought we would be able to stop the train full of prisoners and thereby slow the Yeerk infestation of new hosts?

Our next step was clear.

We needed to get out. Quickly.

Rachel came flapping toward me out of the darkness.

James appeared not far behind her, big paws stepping slowly and cautiously along the narrow walkway, shaggy lion's head watching. Observing. There was blood on his jowls and paws.

<The Hork-Bajir took off down tunnel,> he said. <Limping, actually. I didn't stop him but I managed to slow him down.>

Rachel landed on the ground with a flourish of her soft-feathered wings. <Good job, James. You, too, Ax.>

<I think we have done what we came in to accomplish,> I said.

<Are you kidding?> Rachel argued. <We've got the Yeerks on the run! We're right here in the tunnel! Let's do some serious damage!>

I tried to keep my voice from showing my impatience. And I resolved to tell Jake that Rachel was unfit for missions without him. Her eagerness to fight was getting to be too much.

<Rachel, there are only three of us,> I said reasonably. <And I think we would do better to learn more about this operation before we strike again with a larger and more prepared force.>

Rachel's large owl eyes blinked. I could not tell if her response was hostile or thoughtful.

<Okay,> she said after a long silence. <You're right. I'm going Hork-Bajir. Follow the group that

went down the tunnel and see what I can find out. I'll just see what I can see. I won't fight. Give me half an hour.>

I said nothing.

<That *okay* with you, Ax?> she asked. Now I heard definite antagonism in her voice.

<I am not in charge,> I said shortly. <If you choose to investigate further, that is your decision.>

There was a long pause.

James finally spoke. <Ax is right. We need to be careful. You go Hork-Bajir, Rachel. See what you can find out. But we'll wait here. Just in case.>

<If I don't come back, don't come after me,> Rachel said unnecessarily.

We would not.

The resistance could not afford to lose even one member now. And certainly not three. We shouldn't have been in the subway station in the first place.

We had not even managed to stop one trainload of prisoners. And undoubtedly there were many tunnels and many trains.

We had done nothing but put the enemy on high alert. And endangered our own lives.

I wished now not for Jake, but for an Andalite commander. An experienced soldier. Someone who better understood when to fight and when to watch.

Someone who understood tactics.

Someone who understood me.

I watched silently as Rachel morphed. As she trotted awkwardly along the tunnel's narrow walkway into the darkness beyond.

And I sincerely hoped for her safe return.

CHAPTER 7

Three hours later we were back at camp.

All of us.

It was late afternoon and the sun was setting behind the canopy of trees that kept our camp from being seen from above.

Camp consisted of a muddy, wooded, and heavily guarded compound built by a colony of free Hork-Bajir. Rebel Hork-Bajir who had escaped the tyranny of the Yeerks and had gone into hiding.

Their leader was Toby.

When the Yeerks discovered the true identity of the resistance we, the Animorphs, evacuated our homes immediately.

Now the muddy and primitive camp is full, crowded, and contentious.

There are the free Hork-Bajir.

But there are also humans.

There is Marco, his father, and his mother, Eva, who was once host body of the former Visser One. That Yeerk is now dead and Eva is free. Reunited with her husband and her son.

Living with Marco's parents is a young girl named Elena who is blind when not in morph. Rachel gave her the morphing technology and allowed Elena to acquire her. Our mission to recruit several children from a school for the blind failed. Elena managed to escape the Yeerks in her Rachel morph. Now she lives as a refugee and cannot, for security reasons, return to the school or her parents. She is sad for her losses but slowly adjusting to her new life.

Also in the camp are Cassie and her parents, Michelle and Walter, both veterinarians. Tobias and his mother, Loren, too. Loren has no memory of Tobias's father, Elfangor. My brother.

And there is Rachel's mother, Naomi, and Rachel's two younger sisters, Sara and Jordan.

Rachel's mother is quite quarrelsome. I am told that is because she is something called a "lawyer." A lawyer seems to be an odd type of human. Intelligent but in a way that is not terri-

bly useful. At least to my Andalite sensibilities. All they seem to use their intellect for is argument. Not philosophical contemplation or artistic pursuit.

I am told that although people often find themselves in need of a lawyer, lawyers are not very popular. After the last few days, I understand why.

Lastly, there is Jake.

Jake's family is not in our camp. Jake's brother, Tom, has been a Controller from the early days of the invasion. Recently, Jake's parents were captured by the Yeerks — with Tom's help — and made into human-Controllers.

This has made Jake very withdrawn. For a time he said he did not want to lead us anymore. Our morale suffered.

Now, after our last confrontation with Tom, during which we lost the morphing cube to the Yeerks, Jake is beginning to take charge again. He is still somewhat depressed and often angry. But as he listened to Rachel's report his face showed interest.

"The Yeerks used what they had. They extended the existing subway tunnels using Taxxon labor," Rachel was telling him. "We know what effective diggers Taxxons are. Now the trains run all the way to the main pool. My estimate is that there are at least six lines leading to it. And I spotted some Taxxons at work on what looked like another new line."

"When you think how fast the Yeerks can move hundreds, maybe thousands of people in and out of the central pool . . ."

James did not need to finish his sentence. We all understood the implications of the Yeerks' newest scheme.

With that kind of rapid expansion system in place in cities throughout the world, the Yeerks could rule Earth in what would seem like no time at all.

"They're probably bringing in transports of unhosted Yeerks," Marco said grimly. "Why should the Yeerks stay on their own planet when they can take over this one, have an unlimited supply of hosts, and pretty much unimpeded access to a feeding pool?"

<So, we're dead?> Tobias said.

Toby, who was sitting in with us, shook her head. "Not necessarily. If the Yeerks are concentrating here, on this planet, around this pool, then . . ."

Marco grinned. "Right. They can move Yeerks in in big numbers. But we can take them out in big numbers."

"How?" Rachel asked eagerly.

"A subway train loaded with explosives," Marco said. "A small nuke if we could get our

hands on one. Run that puppy at full speed, detonate it in the Yeerk pool, big BOOM! 'Bye-'bye Yeerks."

Cassie took a deep breath before she spoke. "You can't be serious."

"Why not?" Rachel.

Cassie looked at Jake. Jake looked away.

"Think! Those trains are full of people being taken to the Yeerk pool for infestation. We'd be killing thousands of Yeerks, yes. But we'd also be killing thousands of people who want nothing more than to go home and forget any of this ever happened."

<We've been down this path before,> Tobias agreed. <Cassie's right. We're supposed to be saving humanity. Not slaughtering people who have the bad luck to get in the way.> He looked pointedly at Marco. <Think about it. Your mom could still be down there.>

Marco lowered his eyes. But only for a moment. Then he lifted them and looked at Jake.

We all looked at Jake.

His brother. His mother. His father. Any of them. All of them. Tom could be stationed at that Yeerk pool. Jake's parents, low-level, unwilling Controllers, could be trapped down there in cages while their Yeerks fed on Kandrona.

Jake's face turned pale. "I'm not making this decision. It has to be a vote."

Rachel stood and looked angrily around the circle of faces. "You're kidding, right? I mean, you think saving the earth really demands a vote?"

"The ends simply don't justify the means," Cassie said softly.

Rachel glared angrily at her. "You weren't there," she said. "You didn't see what we saw. It was like some old World War Two newsreel or something. People being rounded up and forced at gunpoint onto trains. Men, women, old people, and kids. It's like the Yeerks don't even care anymore about finding the healthiest and strongest to infest. They're taking everyone. Quantity over quality."

Cassie waved her hands in frustration. "Exactly. And those are the people you would kill while you're trying to stop the Yeerks. Little kids. Retirees. Someone's grandparents."

"You know, we won't actually be using a nuke," Marco said quietly. "Not that that changes things much," he admitted.

There was a long, long silence. I could see each one of them grappling with his or her conscience.

Toby stared stolidly into space. Her home planet had been through a devastating war with the Yeerks. Most of her people had not survived. The majority of the ones who had were now Hork-

Bajir-Controllers. A smaller number of survivors or children of survivors were here in the camp.

Frankly, I did not know what her vote would be. I could not read her inscrutable expression.

But I knew that, like me, Toby understood that she was an outsider here on Earth. That her ideas and experiences were her own. And that she often did not understand human thought processes or emotions.

I was surprised when she spoke. "This is a war," she said quietly. "There is no question that people will die. The only question is, who?"

There was another long pause.

<Okay,> Tobias said finally. <I guess that sort of sums it up.> He was trying to sound unconcerned but his voice quivered.

Rachel's voice, on the other hand, was firm and unhesitating. "I don't know about you guys, but I'm thinking it's time to explode a big 'ole bomb."

"And you couldn't be happier," Cassie said bitterly to Rachel. "Could you?"

CHAPTER 8

Two hours later we were still strategizing. Marco was correct in stating that nuclear weapons, fairly primitive explosives by Andalite standards, are very difficult for the average citizen to procure.

This is a good thing.

It wasn't that long ago when we had just barely succeeded in averting a Yeerk-instigated World War III. There was a fierce battle on board a United States Navy aircraft carrier. Many, many innocent American men and women were killed. And it was likely that the few survivors were traumatized by the brutal attack of Yeerk-infested humans and battalions of Hork-Bajir- and Taxxon-Controllers.

Near the end of that horrible battle I had not listened to Jake. I had even gone so far as to knock him unconscious so that I could carry out a desperate plan without interference. A plan that seemed to me the only way to a possible victory.

My actions were in some ways traitorous. But in other ways, they were necessary.

Against express orders I kidnapped Visser Two and commandeered an F-14D Tomcat. The Yeerks had fitted out the plane with a nuclear weapon. Once in the air with my captive I threatened to drop the nuclear weapon directly over the Yeerk pool. The result of such an action would have been not only the utter destruction of the pool complex itself, but also severe damage to my friends' community and the inevitable loss of thousands of human lives.

It was a calculated risk, a terrible gamble. Threaten to kill thousands to save millions, maybe billions. Thankfully, my plan worked. Visser Two agreed to call off the planned nuclear strike against China if I would promise not to drop a bomb on the Yeerk pool.

Would I have followed through on my threat if Visser Two had not complied? Could I have?

To this day I have no answer to either of those questions.

Now, here we were, not long after the very public incident on the USS *George Washington*, just days from the governor's televised warning, once again discussing the total destruction of the Yeerks' main feeding operation.

We sat by a low campfire, studying a map of the county spread out on an old picnic table.

We were minus James, who had gone back to the hospital where he lived. It was essential for the new recruits to remain undercover for as long as possible. We were also minus Toby. She had been asked to help settle a dispute between one of the older Hork-Bajir and Rachel's mother.

Marco pointed to a military base on the map. "This place might be storing nuclear weapons. But like I said before, even if we managed to get in past security and steal a nuke, we wouldn't be able to use it. It would take us too long to figure out its security codes. Way elaborate. By the time we knew what we were doing, the military would know what we were doing, too."

"What if we had help from the Chee?" Jake asked.

Tobias blinked fiercely. <The Chee won't help us. Not with something like this. Something overtly aggressive.>

The Chee are a race of androids who live here on Earth. They are incredibly brilliant. And their technical capabilities are more advanced even than those of the Andalites.

However, the Chee are hard-wired pacifists.

They will help us defend ourselves. But they would never help us with an assault.

"Tobias is right. The Chee won't help us," Jake mused. "Everything about this idea is against who they are and what they're all about."

"Back to the problem," Marco continued. "We don't really even need a nuke. We'll go with garden-variety explosives."

Jake lifted an eyebrow. "Such as?"

Marco shrugged. "Such as dynamite. Okay. Look." Marco pointed to a red circle on the map. "This is a National Guard installation. They do a lot of roadwork, forestry, and fire fighting in the national parks. Other public works. That means they've probably got some sort of armory, stores of dynamite, maybe other explosives."

"I'm sure potentially dangerous materials like dynamite and bombs are under pretty heavy lock and key," Cassie pointed out. "We're still going to have to get past all sorts of security."

Marco shrugged. "Hey. I never said it was going to be easy. All I'm saying is that if we can get hold of enough dynamite, we could pack a train with it and ram the pool. Put some major hurt on the Yeerks."

Jake nodded. "Yeah. The question is how."

"We've got some friends in the National Guard, don't we?" Cassie asked.

Marco frowned. <Do we? We don't know for

sure that Lieutenant Colonel Larsen is still with the governor. I mean, where is he while all of this Yeerk movement is going down? Where's the governor? For that matter, where's our buddy Collins? Guy took a Dracon to the shoulder and still refused to go off duty. I wouldn't mind him on our team right about now.>

<Yeah.> Jake nodded. <Good guys. But I'm not sure we can count on our old allies anymore. Something tells me they've probably been taken. Let's face it. The governor seriously ticked off Visser One.>

<So who can we count on? Okay, maybe we'll run into an uninfested National Guard commander, but maybe not. Who do we have for sure?> Tobias mused.

"Us. And I mean all of us," Rachel said excitedly. "The six of us. James and the new guys. Parents. Toby and what Hork-Bajir soldiers she can spare. It'll be the most major operation we've launched so far."

"That's the entire resistance," Jake said.

"Risking the whole team on one mission." Cassie.

There was a long pause.

<You know, maybe we should rethink this,> Tobias said.

"Yeah, we should," Cassie agreed. "This mission is way too heavy with bad karma."

Jake turned on her angrily. "Look, Cassie, it would be nice if we had more choices. But now that the Yeerks have morphing technology, we've lost our major edge. Which means that now we have to take some major unpleasant risks."

His voice was angry. Sarcastic. Accusatory.

I had never heard Jake speak that way to anyone.

And since his friendship with Cassie is quite special, his tone was even more surprising.

Cassie looked stricken. I wondered if she would answer him with equal passion. But she did not. Instead, she looked as if she might cry.

The others looked at one another, bewildered. It was almost as if Jake were blaming Cassie for the Yeerk acquisition of morphing technology.

I shifted my weight from one leg to the other and observed the humans around me.

Relationships were changing.

Loyalties were shifting.

There were unspoken animosities and hidden agendas.

The decisions were becoming more about emotions than tactics. The resistance was jeopardizing its ability to be effective.

I had been told this might happen.

CHAPTER 9

Late that night I took the Z-space transponder.

It was necessary to avoid detection by any of the camp's inhabitants.

It was also necessary to avoid detection by any Yeerk spies.

Since the Yeerks had taken the morphing technology, any animal spotted in the camp or its environs was suspect. Every singing bird a potential enemy. Any scurrying vole a possible traitor to our cause.

Therefore, each of us had acquired several additional morphs native to the camp's wooded mountain environment. We routinely used these common, largely innocuous morphs to get about

at night or when we had to leave the camp's perimeters. At night, a lone Animorph was more vulnerable to attack. But just as we could not attack and kill every living creature that passed through the camp, neither could a Yeerk in morph attack and kill every waddling woodchuck or slithering snake.

Clouds covered the moon. I took advantage of the almost total darkness and quickly morphed a raccoon. I was able to leave the camp without any Hork-Bajir or human lookout spotting me. An adult female raccoon with a piece of alien technology wedged in her mouth.

I scurried off into the night. I would not have much time and I did not want to bring the Yeerks too close to the camp.

As soon as I reached what I considered to be a safe distance, I removed the Z-space transponder from my mouth and activated it. The raccoon's small and dexterous "hands" were strangely similar to those of an Andalite and were perfectly suited to the task. The morph had become a new favorite of mine.

I listened as the waves warped and wove through galaxies, finding their way to the Andalite home planet.

After a short delay, there was a response. Coded, yes. But a code that had been carefully worked out. Numeric but thoughtspoken.

<Aximili-Esgarrouth-Isthill?>

<Yes.> I gave the password to clear the channel for communication.

<Report,> came the curt command.

<It is just as you predicted,> I told Jaham-Estalan-Forlan, a war prince and chief of the Andalite military. <The human resistance is rapidly losing its effectiveness. There is infighting. Tensions. Discipline is breaking down.>

<They know nothing of our previous communications?>

<They know nothing,> I confirmed.

<Good.>

<The Yeerk concentration here is escalating. They are forcibly transporting thousands of humans to the central Yeerk pool via the subway system. In retaliation, the resistance is planning the destruction of that central pool.>

Jaham-Estalan-Forlan made a sound of impatience. <Do they truly believe they can defeat the Yeerks by destroying only one central pool?>

I felt a need to defend my friends. <It is all they can do — for now.> Then I realized my defense would only increase Jaham-Estalan-Forlan's contempt for the human race. He would think that if the resistance could muster no better defense than my excuse-making, they would not be worth saving.

<The high command has met and made their

decision. If the Yeerks are indeed concentrating on the planet Earth, we must allow their plan to continue. Once the bulk of the Yeerk race has been transported, the planet can be quarantined.>

Quarantined.

A polite word for consigning the human race to a life of slavery under the Yeerks.

I thought about Jake. The others. Tobias. After all our time together, I felt affection for them.

<Aximili? Did you hear me?>

Yes, I felt affection. But I was still an Andalite. I was still a soldier. And this was still a war.

<I heard,> I responded.

<Do nothing to hamper the Yeerk concentration on Earth. Stop the resistance's attack on the pool. We must let the Yeerks believe they have won. Do you understand?>

I did.

Would Jake?

Would the others?

Never.

<Once the planet is quarantined,> War Prince Jaham continued, <we will be in a position to negotiate. We will mediate a peaceful symbiosis between humans and Yeerks.>

I wondered if this was an accurate description of the Andalite high command's intention.

The high command might disdain the humans, but they knew from my reports that humans were very ingenious. Very determined. Very tenacious.

Millions of Yeerks with human hosts would constitute an intolerable threat.

A quarantine would never hold. Not even if every ship in the Andalite fleet were assigned to police the perimeters of Earth's atmosphere.

The Yeerk-human axis would push out. And it would conquer everything in its path.

<Has there been any change in technology acquisition?> Jaham-Estalan-Forlan asked.

I knew I should tell him that the Yeerks were now in posession of morphing technology. But I did not. <No,> I said.

Perhaps I would tell the truth later. I wanted time to consider. To think how such a revelation would affect the Andalite high command's plans for the planet.

It was an undisciplined decision, my decision to withhold the truth. It was not my place to second-guess the decisions of my superiors. Perhaps I had been on Earth too long.

Suddenly I could hear Bug fighters in the distance, drawn to the signals they had picked up from the Z-space transponder.

Quickly I severed the connection and began to demorph and remorph to horned owl, an excel-

lent form of night transport. The Zero-space transponder was small enough to carry in my talons.

By the time the Bug fighters were hovering over my previous position, I was winging my way unseen back to camp.

Quarantine.

Quarantine.

Quarantine.

It was just a way of saying what could not be said over any channel of communication, no matter how secure. Because it was something that could not even be said in the chambers of the high command.

The stated goal would be to quarantine.

The orders would say to quarantine.

But what everyone would understand is that a quarantine would be impossible to sustain.

To enforce a quarantine, the Andalite fleet would be forced to engage.

And once they engaged, they would annihilate the planet and every living thing on it. Yeerk and human.

Quarantine was the first step toward genocide.

The high command had made its decision. The Yeerk conquest of the galaxy would stop here on Earth.

The camp came into view. I wished I could

just keep going. Perhaps become a *nothlit.* Be free of the terrible burdens of secrecy and betrayal.

I remembered the Yeerk falcon. Five minutes away from freedom.

But the price of that freedom was high.

Maybe too high.

CHAPTER 10

The next morning, Jake gathered us together to finalize our plans.

The Animorphs were there, Tobias in human form. Toby was there. James was there on behalf of the new recruits. And Marco's parents were present.

"I've been on the computer all night," Marco said. "All of us. Me, Mom, and Dad. We hacked into nearly every file on the National Guard base. Bottom line? They've got a big warehouse full of thousand-pound bombs."

"Yes!" Rachel grinned. "Major firepower."

Marco's mother looked exhausted. "We could kill a lot of slugs with one thousand-pound bomb."

"We could kill them all with ten or twelve thousand-pound bombs," Marco's dad amended. "In an enclosed space an explosion of even one thousand-pound bomb would have incredible magnitude. The devastation would be close to that of an atomic explosion."

Rachel nodded with satisfaction. "We'd be going seriously medieval on Yeerk butt."

"The big question is: How?" Jake asked. "We talked about this before. We'd have to commit everything. Everybody. Animorphs, all of us. Hork-Bajir. Parents."

"I'm out," Cassie said hotly. "I thought that maybe . . . But I can't. And I can tell you my parents are out, too."

Rachel glared at her. "Okay, Cassie," she said in a sarcastic-sweet tone. "So, what do you think we should do instead? Just sit here and wait for the Yeerks to find us? Or maybe we should make it real easy on them and all go hop on the train for a little swim in the pool."

"Why do you have to be so horrible?" Cassie exploded. "You are, you know. And you get worse every day. Your own mother can't even stand you."

Cassie turned to walk away, but Jake grabbed her sleeve. "Cassie! Come on."

"Come on what!" Cassie spit. "You don't knowingly take innocent life. Not if you're a de-

cent person. Not if you're not a murderer. The goal is irrelevant. I thought you knew that, Jake, but apparently . . ."

"Apparently you decided to start making decisions for me!" Jake shouted back. "Somewhere along the line you decided that you knew what was best. For me. For everybody. Well, guess what?"

Cassie put her hands in front of her as if she were going to shove Jake away. "Don't. Stop! Just don't. Please."

The rest of the assembled group was silent. I believe it is safe to say that none of us understood what was causing Jake and Cassie to argue so furiously.

Tears began to roll down Cassie's cheeks. "I'm sorry," she said. "I shouldn't have done it. I don't even really know why I did it. I . . . At that moment it seemed the right thing to do. The only thing. Now, I'm just sorry. I'm sorry."

"What is she talking about?" Marco whispered.

"It was me!" Cassie shouted. "I gave the Yeerks the morphing cube. I let Tom run away with it. I stopped Jake from chasing him. From killing him. Me!"

I felt my back legs weaken slightly.

Cassie? A traitor?

It did not seem possible.

"Oh, Cassie," Eva murmured.

"You did what?!" Marco said, his voice hoarse.

"Tom had it. He had the cube. The only way Jake was going to get it from him was to kill him. I couldn't let Jake do that. I couldn't. I was trying to protect him."

"You were trying to protect Jake so you basically sold out the rest of the human race?" Rachel said. Her voice was tight. The voice of controlled ferocity. Violence just barely contained.

"I'm sure she didn't think of it in those terms," Tobias said softly.

"I didn't think at all," Cassie said, her voice exhausted and full of grief. "It was more of an impulse. An instinct. Something inside just told me to let Tom take the cube. I knew . . . I knew I was making a sacrifice. That I was sacrificing so much . . . maybe now it seems stupid. But at that moment I thought I was doing the right thing. I really did."

Rachel lifted her hand. Began to make a fist. Tobias grabbed her wrist.

And surprisingly, Jake pulled Cassie to him and embraced her.

Cassie leaned her head on his shoulder.

Jake pressed his cheek against her hair. "It's okay, Cassie," he said, his voice ragged. "I'm sorry. It's okay."

Embarrassed, I averted my eyes.

After several moments Cassie withdrew from Jake's arms and faced the rest of us. "I am so sorry. I made a mistake. A terrible mistake. I won't do it again. I won't try to decide what's right for everyone. It was arrogant and dangerous. I didn't mean it to be but it was."

Jake ran his hands through his hair. "Look. This is hard stuff. But we've got to work as a team. We don't have room for individual agendas. We go or we don't go. But either way . . ."

Jake's voice droned on. But I was no longer listening.

I could not stop looking at Cassie.

I was not exactly sure what I was feeling.

But I was sure it was very close to hatred.

CHAPTER 11

Toby spoke in her guttural voice. "My people are tired of hiding. We are a peaceful species. But we will fight. It is better than always living in fear."

"I'm with Toby," Marco said. "Dad? Mom?"

Marco's mother nodded grimly. "I've had the worst of the Yeerk high command living in my head. I know there's no appeasement. My advice is to fight. Go in. Clean house. Do as much damage as we can. Visser One does not cope well with setbacks. If we do enough damage, we could possibly chase the Yeerks off Earth."

"What do you mean?" Jake asked.

"The former Visser One didn't advocate all-out war because she knew Earth was too volatile.

The inhabitants too resistant. The Yeerks are used to tractable host bodies. Humans are a fighting race. They fight invaders. They fight each other. They don't give up easily. The current Visser One has never really understood that."

"So?" Jake pressed.

"So, knowing something about the Yeerk High Council, I'm thinking it's likely Visser One's been warned that one more major attack on a site of concentration, or one more major disaster like what happened on the aircraft carrier, or one more public announcement by the governor calling for resistance, just might mean the end of his domination here. It might mean the Yeerks would decide to move their base of operations to some other planet. Let's face it. With the ability to morph, the Yeerks don't really need humans. They could make do with another species on another planet, a species less aggressive than humans."

There was a long silence.

"I'm not sure that's good news for the rest of the world," Jake commented.

"But it's good news for us. Earth is Visser One's personal fiefdom," Marco's father said. "If the Yeerks are forced to leave Earth, Visser One's back to being a subvisser somewhere."

"We may not be able to defeat the Yeerks, but

we can at least move them off Earth," Marco said.

"And inflict them on another species?" Cassie.

Toby's eyes narrowed. "Perhaps not. With help from the Andalite fleet, perhaps we could keep the Yeerks from settling anywhere."

"What do you mean?" Rachel asked.

"We chase them into Zero-space and the Andalite fleet ambushes them there. Effectively wipes them out."

Jake's eyes narrowed as he considered the possibility. "We don't know what we can count on from the Andalite fleet, as long as the Yeerks are Earth's problem. But maybe Toby's right. If we can chase the Yeerks off Earth and make them the Andalites' problem, the Andalites would be forced to act. Ax?"

My hearts thundered. I felt ill with anger. And something close to guilt. <It is hard to know what the Andalite high command would order,> I said, my voice cold.

"Fair enough," Jake said. But he gave me an odd look. "In any event, step one is to blow the Yeerk pool."

I said nothing.

Should I have told the high command everything?

Yes. I should have. Without doubt.

They needed to know that the entire situation on Earth was changing.

Because of one human.

Because of Cassie.

Of course, it has always been a possibility that the enemy might somehow acquire morphing technology, either through conquest or guile. War is about losses as well as victories.

But to surrender without struggle your most important piece of technology . . . strategy . . . defense . . . It was simply incomprehensible to me.

It was also incomprehensible to me that Cassie was allowed to participate in this discussion.

On my own planet, she would have been tried for treason and executed immediately.

And yet, the others continued to consult her.

My hatred for Cassie began to extend to them all. They were fools. They would never prevail. They were too soft. Too sentimental. Too childish. Too stupid and ignorant.

Stupidity and ignorance within one's own ranks are more dangerous opponents than an outside enemy could ever be. I had been taught that lesson in the military academy. Now I had been given an object lesson that proved the principle.

As the humans continued to plan and plot, my mind raced. I did not know what to do.

Perhaps I should contact War Prince Jaham-Estalan-Forlan and tell him I had been interrupted by Bug fighters before making a full report. I could tell him that the Yeerks had acquired Andalite morphing technology.

And I could tell him that if the Andalite high command was going to quarantine the planet, they needed to do it quickly.

"Let's go back to the attack," Marco said. "Cassie may have been a major idiot for about half a second, but she's right now. If there are innocent people trapped down in the tunnel, how can we justify blowing it up?"

"What if we gave them time to escape," Tobias suggested. "I mean, what if somehow, just before the explosion, we told everyone on site that the pool was about to blow. The humans and the human-Controllers would probably run for their lives. The Yeerks in their heads will starve without the pool, but the humans would live. See? We save the humans, kill the Yeerks, and wipe out a major infestation center."

Marco nodded. "That works for me. I mean, at least it gives people a chance. Some of them, anyway."

One by one, each of the group nodded. Each signaled his or her approval of the plan.

Each person but Cassie. She stared at the ground. Her cheeks were stained with tears.

No one seemed to know what to say to her.

Finally, Jake spoke. "Cassie?"

Cassie shook her head. "I'll do whatever you guys say."

"That's not good enough, Cassie," Jake said. "You've always had definite ideas about what we should or shouldn't do. Don't weasel now."

Cassie lifted her face. "Okay. Then it's wrong. But let's do it anyway. I'll learn to live with my conscience. We all will. I don't have a better plan. I guess this is as close as we'll get to defeating the Yeerks without being the Yeerks."

Jake's face relaxed. I saw the faintest hint of a smile. Almost of relief.

He addressed the group. "Look. Cassie did what she did. She had her reasons. I don't understand them so I can't say if they were right or wrong. But her decision to let Tom get away with the morphing cube changed the equation. Still, I trust Cassie's instincts. Even more than my own. Especially my own these days. So let's just readopt this phrase as our guideline. Defeat the Yeerks. Don't become them."

He did not look directly at Rachel, but I knew he was telling her to restrain her violent impulses.

I remembered again the desperate falcon. The one who yearned for freedom. Had he found it in the sky, or in death?

For a long time, I have regarded Rachel as representing one end of the continuum of human nature. What all humans would become if the war went on long enough.

That perception has guided many of my decisions.

An entire human race of Rachels — angry, merciless, aggressive, and equipped with Yeerk and Andalite technology. It was a terrifying specter.

But perhaps . . . perhaps I had been wrong.

Perhaps the real menace lay at the other end of the continuum — represented by Cassie. Humans who were softer. Kinder. Well-meaning.

And, ironically, infinitely more dangerous.

CHAPTER 12

That night, I asked Cassie if I might speak with her privately.

She was subdued. Still shaken after our meeting. "Let's go sit somewhere quiet and dark," she said.

We walked together to the far perimeter of the camp. A free Hork-Bajir sat high up in a tree branch keeping watch. But he paid little attention to us.

Cassie folded her arms across her chest and sighed.

<Tell me about the morphing cube,> I said. <Why did you keep Jake from chasing Tom?>

"Look, Ax. I already feel like a criminal. Okay?

But I've already made my apologies. Why do I have to go through this again with you?"

I was angry. So angry the blade on my tail was quivering. <Because my brother, Elfangor, gave the cube to you. To you and your friends. He compromised everything he stood for by giving it to you. He betrayed the laws of his own people. He placed his trust in five humans. I am trying to understand why you would betray him in return. Why you would betray your friends. And why you would betray your people.>

They were harsh words.

But I had a right to say those harsh words. Because it was my brother, my people, and my planet's technology that had been abused.

According to Cassie, she had sacrificed them all on no more than an instinct. An impulse.

I had to think there was a better reason.

If not, then I could not help but believe that the high command had every right to annihilate this planet. And I would tell them so tonight.

Humans were a retrograde species — destructive, violent, and at the mercy of their emotions. Unable to make personal sacrifices or set aside personal agendas on behalf of a larger cause.

Cassie's head dropped. She put her hands over her face. "Oh, Ax, you're right." Her voice

broke. "I did betray Elfangor. I never thought about how you would feel."

<No,> I agreed coldly. <I am still trying to understand what it was you *did* think.>

Cassie rubbed her temples, as if she were struggling with memories she would prefer to suppress. "I suppose . . . I suppose . . ."

She stared at me, almost fearfully. "It wasn't just about Tom. It wasn't just about Jake."

<Then what was it about? What did you think you were doing?>

"Ax," she whispered, as one about to voice a terrible secret. "I just know there are so many Yeerks who would defect if they could. Aftran wasn't the only one, we know that. There's always been a group of Yeerks who can't stand the notion of infestation. Who don't want to be parasites. Who don't want to be slavish followers of the vissers! Remember the first battle with the new recruits, when Visser One was in that horrible morph and choking Jake to death? Remember how that Hork-Bajir cut off one of the visser's tentacles and freed Jake? Some of the Yeerks just want to be free! Now, with the ability to morph, maybe they can be. We can't fight on forever. Not just us. And it's beginning to look as if we can't win by conquering. We may just have to learn to coexist. I don't know what was in my head at that moment, when I let Tom go. But now, in retrospect, maybe letting the Yeerks have the morphing technology is the way to peace."

My back legs felt as if they might collapse. For one person to make a decision so momentous and act on it without first talking to anyone . . . It was unthinkable.

And yet my conscience nagged uncomfortably. Hadn't I acted similarly? Hadn't I acted without the permission of my prince? Hadn't I assumed the right to take an enormous risk with human lives when I commandeered the plane fitted out with a nuclear weapon, kidnapped Visser Two, and threatened to explode the bomb directly over the Yeerk pool? Such an explosion would have destroyed most if not all of my friends' hometown and most if not all of its citizens.

The memory was too troubling. I chased it away and reached wildly for a way to continue to separate myself from Cassie.

Perhaps Jake had known what Cassie was going to do. Suspicion grew in my hearts. <Does Jake agree with this assessment?> I asked coldly.

Cassie shook her head. "No. No. I haven't told anyone any of this. I can't. Can you imagine what the others would say? Can't you just hear Rachel?

"My god. She lives for the war. And Marco's mom? She hates the Yeerks so much that the

idea of sharing the planet with them makes her physically ill."

<She knows the enemy,> I pointed out. <She knows them in a way we never will. If we continue to be lucky.>

"Of course she feels that way," Cassie said impatiently. "Marco's mother was host to the former Visser One. It must have been horrible. But the former Visser One was one Yeerk. The current Visser One is one Yeerk."

<He is the Yeerks' leader on this planet,> I replied.

"It still doesn't mean he represents each and every Yeerk," Cassie insisted. "Humans have had some pretty evil leaders, too. Thousands, sometimes millions of people have followed those leaders, sometimes willingly, sometimes not. Sometimes because they were just too afraid to say no. What if some other species decided to wipe out the human race based on the existence of a few powerful people? What if that species decided all humans were cruel, based on the actions of a handful of sociopaths?"

In spite of myself, I stumbled over my thoughts.

Cassie gave me a sharp look.

Was she expecting an answer? Or was it a rhetorical question? Either way, it had come too close for comfort.

We stared at each other for a long moment.

<In the tunnel, I caught a falcon,> I told her. <A Yeerk falcon. He begged to be let go. He wanted to stay in morph. To live to escape.>

Cassie nodded slowly. "You see? I'm right."

I shook my head. "No. You are wrong. Visser One will learn to control whoever acquires morphing technology. He will give it only to the most loyal Yeerks."

"But the falcon you caught . . ."

"The falcon I caught might have been lying," I said simply. "Or he may truthfully have been seeking escape. Yes, one or two Yeerks may be seduced by the possibility of escape. But not enough."

"Do you think you can forgive me for this?" she said quietly.

<I do not know, Cassie.>

"What are you going to do?"

<I do not know,> I answered again.

"I think this attack on the Yeerk pool will be our last stand. And if the Yeerks get any idea of our plan, any warning at all, chances are none of us will make it out alive," Cassie said.

I shook my head. <I am an Andalite. I will never run away.>

"You think I'm a traitor, don't you?" she asked.

I nodded. <Yes.>

"But did I do the wrong thing?"

<I do not know.>

"How do you think Elfangor would answer that question?"

<I do not know that, either. I wish I did.>

I turned and walked away through the darkness to an area thick with tree trunks and shrubs. I needed to be alone.

No matter what happened, I knew I would never feel quite the same about Cassie.

Or any other human.

CHAPTER 13

I stared upward, trying to glimpse the stars through the thick canopy of trees.

My birthplace was somewhere out there. I had come to believe I would never see it again. I closed my main eyes, trying to remember it in detail. Trying to remember the faces of my family and friends.

But their faces kept fading away and changing into other faces.

Jake. Rachel. Tobias. Cassie. Marco.

The humans amazed me with their resilience, their ingenuity, and their bravery.

They delighted me with their humor, their passions, and their capacity for play. Their food.

But they truly sickened me with their self-indulgence and their childishness.

But then, I reminded myself, they are children. And so am I.

If I were at home, I would still be a cadet in the Andalite Military Academy. I would spend most of my time in my parents' scoop.

But I had been thrust into the midst of this raging war on Earth.

I had seen more battles, death, and destruction than many seasoned soldiers in our Andalite fleet.

I felt my throat tighten and constrict. My hearts ached with a pain I could not describe. I wondered if I were dying.

I felt not sadness. I felt pity. For myself. For us all. We were children no longer. And we never would be again.

"What do you think Elfangor would say?" It was if Cassie had looked into my mind and read the question there.

Elfangor! Why did you have to die and leave me here? I do not know what to do.

Either path led me to betrayal.

Elfangor was a great hero. A war prince. A member of the Andalite military. Brave. When necessary, ruthless.

The Yeerks had to be stopped. The Andalite

high command knew that. Their plans might be unspoken. But they were clear. Annihilation of the planet. It would be clean. It would be final. It would be over.

But . . . but Elfangor had broken the most fundamental law of our planet. He had broken the Law of *Seerow's Kindness.* He had given morphing technology to another species.

To humans.

Why?

To give them a chance?

No. The Elfangor I knew was not sentimental. He would not compromise the safety of the home planet and the galaxy to save one species.

Elfangor knew what every other Andalite knew. That the Yeerk menace had started with an old fool's sentimental impulse. His inability to understand that his enemy's goals and aspirations were not his own.

Seerow had let loose a plague of Yeerks upon the galaxy. The rest is history. A sad, violent, destructive history of conquest and war.

Planets ravaged and ruined.

One species after another enslaved.

Countless dead.

All triggered by an act of kindness.

Yes. The Cassies of the world were infinitely more dangerous than the Rachels.

My brother had known this. So what had possessed him to give these human youths the power to change the future of the galaxy?

What would he tell me to do now?

I heard a flutter of wings. Then, the long quiet sound of studied stillness.

Tobias.

He had settled on a branch. He said nothing for a long time. Then, finally, <Well?>

<Well, what?> I asked.

<What did you decide?>

I was startled. But I tried to pretend I was not. <About what?>

Tobias ruffled his feathers placidly. <I followed you last night. I don't know who you were talking to. Or what you were saying. But I'm guessing you were talking to the Andalite home planet. Am I right?>

I could not lie to my true *shorm*. <Yes.>

<They're going to fry us, aren't they?>

CHAPTER 14

My eye stalks waved in spite of my determination to stay calm. <What makes you think that?>

<It's what makes sense for them to do now that the Yeerks are concentrated on Earth. I guess the question is, are you going to help them do it?>

<I do not know. I do not know what is the right thing to do.>

<There's a lot of that going around,> Tobias said.

<Do you hate Cassie?> I asked suddenly.

<I don't hate anybody,> Tobias said calmly. <It's strange, but right now, I don't even hate the Yeerks. It's like, they're trying to survive. And

we're trying to survive. I'm not really sure why it has to be an either-or thing.>

<You would consider a symbiotic truce?>

<No. But we probably wouldn't have to do that. Don't you see? What do the Yeerks need? Bodies. If they can morph bodies from their slug state then . . . they don't have to keep taking other people's bodies as hosts. See? They'd have to deal with the two-hour time limit still. And they'd still have to feed on Kandrona. But . . .>

So. Tobias and Cassie had been thinking similar thoughts.

<But the Yeerks would want to acquire humans. Other sentient creatures, as well. Not just cats and dogs.>

<Yeah?>

<But we have always said it is wrong. Especially without first receiving the person's permission. I cannot imagine a Yeerk asking permission to acquire a human's DNA. And I cannot imagine many humans who would freely give their DNA to a Yeerk.>

Tobias adjusted his wings and appeared to tighten his talons on the branch. <Maybe you're right. I don't know. Look, Ax, it's a whole new world. We're having to make all this up as we go along. There aren't any rules falling out of the sky telling us what and what not to do.>

<What exactly do you mean?>

<Too hard to explain right now,> Tobias said. <I just mean that we don't really have any time-tested rules for dealing with these issues. Like the morality of acquiring someone's DNA. So we have to see what works and what doesn't. We can't afford to get so locked into one idea that we defend it to the death, without really knowing if that idea works — in the real world.>

Tobias was silent for a moment, then flapped away.

My hearts raced. New possibilities were unfolding. New solutions.

Maybe Elfangor had seen something. A possibility that had seemed impossible because we Andalites had been so indoctrinated by our own military thinking. Us versus the enemy. No compromise.

We had decided long ago that morphing was proprietary. Too dangerous to share. But maybe Cassie had been right after all. Maybe the way to real peace was in giving choices to other species.

On the other hand, maybe it depended on the species.

Humans.

Yeerks.

If each were freed from the fight for survival, would they use the morphing technology for good or for evil?

The high command had ordered me to stop the attack on the Yeerk pool. It would be simple to do. Just tip off the Yeerks and the mission would abort before it could begin.

But if I assisted the mission, it would delay the ability of the high command to begin quarantine measures.

What would Elfangor do?

I no longer needed to wonder.

He had done it already.

He had given the morphing cube to the humans. And then he had died.

I, too, would place my faith in the humans.

My faith, if not my trust.

And if I died . . .

Well, then, I hoped I would die as nobly as my brother.

I knew that I should check in with high command. But now that my decision had been made, I did not.

I was willing to disobey a direct order. And I was willing to die.

But I was not willing to deceive the Andalites. To tell them I was going to do one thing, and then do another.

I know it's a fine distinction, but I was learning to rationalize. To defend what was indefensible.

It was a very human course of action.

CHAPTER 15

The following night, I led six human adults through the woods. Loren, Tobias's mother, had received the ability to morph, but chose not to use it unless we expressly asked for her help in a battle situation.

It was a wise decision.

Tobias flew overhead thought-speaking directions to me. The adults made as little noise as possible considering they were carrying a collection of battered metal camping equipment.

Jake, Rachel, Marco, and Cassie were in various bird of prey morphs, flying overhead at different levels.

The auxiliary Animorphs were with us, too. James and his two lieutenants, Craig and Erica,

were in charge of leading the group of seventeen. I did not know who was on the ground and who was in the air.

If the mission went wrong, their instructions were to melt away and save themselves. In this way at least some members of the resistance would live to fight another day.

Toby and several free Hork-Bajir traveled silently and gracefully through the trees.

We were a small, motley army stealing through the night on our way to a work site of National Guardsmen.

According to Tobias, four large covered trucks were parked along the highway where a group of what he estimated to be approximately ten National Guardsmen were repairing a broken water line. They worked at night, of course, so as not to disrupt the heavier daytime traffic.

We wanted the trucks.

"How much further?" Rachel's mother demanded angrily.

"Shhhh!" Eva cautioned.

"I can't believe we're doing this," Naomi went on. She had been complaining incessantly since we left base camp.

"We all agreed to be part of this mission," Loren pointed out reasonably. "Let's just keep going and hope for the best."

Rachel's mother came to a stop. Reluctantly,

I ordered the others to stop as well. “Hope for the best?” she repeated. “That’s all you have to offer? Am I the only one of you people worried about our kids?”

I could not help myself from retorting. <You do not need to be afraid on behalf of Rachel,> I told her. <Rachel is the one who frightens others.>

“And that’s supposed to make me feel better?” her mother demanded shrilly. “To know that my oldest, my first child, my little girl, has become some kind of monster? Some kind of bloodthirsty freak?”

<Don’t let her suck you into an argument, Ax,> Tobias said privately. <You’ll never win. You’re about one-fourth of a mile away from the work site. Keep heading east toward the road.>

<I am afraid I must respectfully ask you to remain silent,> I said to Naomi. Her mouth dropped open in surprise but she spoke no more. <Please follow me.> I turned and pressed on, leading the small group of human adults east through the thick woods.

Finally, we reached the road.

Several yards away, we saw a work crew of National Guardsmen. Flares and barricades lined the road for about a mile in either direction. And best of all, there were the four covered trucks.

<Okay, Dad,> Marco said. <Show time.>

Marco's father stumbled forward onto the road. The others followed several feet behind, canteens clanking against flashlights and tin eating utensils.

Startled, the National Guard commander looked up at the group of bedraggled adults.

"Hello! Hello!" Peter called. "Thank god. We thought we'd never find anybody."

The commander cautiously approached Marco's father. Two other Guardsmen stopped their work and stood protectively at the ready. "Sir? Is there a problem?"

Marco's father gestured toward the other adults. "We've been lost in the woods for two days. Night before last, a bear came into our campsite in the middle of the night. We grabbed what we could and ran. And, er, we got lost."

Marco's father did indeed look as if he had been lost in the woods for several days. He was gaunt. His clothes were filthy and torn. His face was dirty and unshaven.

Marco's mother looked even worse than her husband. She wore an old cap pulled low over her forehead. Her face and hands were smudged with the charcoal from a burnt stick. A human-Controller would have had difficulty recognizing the host body of the former Visser One, but it was always possible that some of the National Guardsmen could be Yeerks.

Rachel's mother looked angry and tired. Very much like a woman who was unaccustomed to doing without a morning shower and other amenities of what Rachel called "the yuppie lifestyle."

Cassie's parents were also dressed in appropriately worn clothing. Each wore a small backpack.

And Tobias's mother hung in the rear, eyes lowered, trying to appear frail and timid. Loren was rather delicate in size and stature. But she had successfully survived far too many ordeals ever to be called timid. In my opinion, my brother Elfangor had married a very brave woman.

I stayed back in the woods, watching, communicating with the other Animorphs. <The approach has been made,> I said. <I do not think these particular Guardsmen are Yeerks. They are surprised at the sudden appearance of a group of lost campers. But they do not seem afraid or suspicious.>

The commander in charge signaled for some of his men to stop work and come forward. "Is anybody sick?" he asked Marco's father. "Any signs of dehydration? When was the last time any of you ate?"

Marco's father put his hand to his chest. "I'm having some pains here."

Immediately, Peter was escorted by three Na-

tional Guardsmen to the truck at the front of the convoy. There they made him sit on the ground. One took his pulse. Another offered him water.

Moments later, the third Guardsman had found places in the three trucks for the five other adults. The commander of the group got on the radio and reported back to the base that he and three of his crew would be bringing in six lost campers, one of whom was having chest pains.

And while this was taking place, Hork-Bajir, under the supervision of Jolphimee-Celpik, were quietly dropping from the trees. When the convoy headed off for the base, the Hork-Bajir would silently disable the remaining seven National Guardsmen at work on the water main. Just in case one was a Yeerk determined to get word to his superiors about a suspicious group of lost campers. Jolphimee-Celpik would see that the Guardsmen came to no harm and were safely released when our mission was completed.

Rachel, Jake, Cassie, and Marco landed unseen and quietly demorphed then remorphed.

<It is all going according to plan,> I told Tobias and the others.

"As soon as we get back to base, we'll get you to a doctor," the commander told Marco's father. "Let's move out!"

Moments later, three trucks were rumbling back to the base. The commander and his three

Guardsmen had no idea that in addition to six human adults they were also transporting four other creatures. And being followed through the roadside treetops by seven-foot-tall aliens.

I morphed to harrier and followed the convoy.

<So far so good.> Tobias. <James, are you guys still with us?>

<All seventeen of us. I just took another count.>

<Good,> I said. <I am in harrier morph about half a mile below you, Tobias. Rachel, Jake, and Cassie are traveling as fleas on Marco.>

<Where is Marco, anyway?>

I could see him, but just barely.

He was the gorilla hitching a ride on the back of the last truck.

CHAPTER 16

Just as we had hoped. The commander had called ahead to explain the emergency situation so the small convoy was not required to stop at the base entrance.

The guards waved the trucks right through without a search.

Now we had to hope the Hork-Bajir had been able to drop onto the base from the surrounding trees. We had to hope that James and his team were close by.

The first truck, the one carrying Marco's father, veered to the right toward the medical station.

The other two trucks pulled into a small yard

full of other military and civilian vehicles. The driver of the second truck got out and walked around to the back.

I could not see his face, but I heard his muffled gasp of surprise as a huge bladed creature grabbed him and pulled him away from the truck. Another muffled gasp, followed by a soft thud as the Guardsman was knocked out, lowered to the ground, and dragged off.

The same scenario was played out behind the other truck. The Hork-Bajir had indeed arrived. The commander and one soldier were with Marco's father. The other two soldiers from the work site were safely out of the way.

Then Naomi and Walter calmly walked around to the driver's side of each of the two trucks and got behind the wheel.

<Okay,> I heard Marco say. <It's a big base. If you were a thousand-pound bomb, where would you be?>

<There are twelve warehouses along the southern perimeter of the base,> Tobias said. <Just like on the map Marco downloaded. And I see four more trucks in a motor pool along the western perimeter.>

<We'll check out the motor pool.> James. <Disable any guards. And be ready for you guys to pick up more transports if you need them.>

<Be careful and try not to hurt anybody,> Jake said. <A lot of these Guardsmen are probably innocent.>

<Got it,> James said.

<Okay.> Marco. <I personally am ready to knock down a few doors.>

The two trucks rumbled toward the warehouses.

There was surprisingly little activity on the base. One man and two women coming out of what might have been the mess hall glanced curiously at us but made no move to investigate. But then, it was late. Most of the Guardsmen, those who had not been part of the road crew, were probably in their barracks.

<We're demorphing,> Rachel said. <I have to tell you, Marco. You stink. Even to the flea you're stinky.>

<You know, Rachel,> he replied, <you —>

<Come on, you two,> I heard Jake say. <Just remorph to firepower as fast as you can. You, too, Ax. I'm going tiger.>

The two trucks pulled around behind the last warehouse. From my vantage point, it seemed the guards in front of Warehouse L took no particular notice.

<Two guards in front of Warehouse A,> Tobias said. <Looks like two guards in front of each of the twelve warehouses.>

<We start the search at A, work our way to L,> Jake called. <But I want all guards incapacitated at the same time, before we start. Does everybody hear me?>

<I'll send Tuan and a few others to help,> James replied.

<Good. Ax, you, Rachel, and Marco take Warehouse A. Tuan, you back them up. As soon as you've knocked out the guards, every team do the same, knock out their guards.>

Jake proceeded to assign teams to Warehouses C through L.

<Let's go, Ax-man.> Rachel.

I landed in the shadows and began to demorph. <I will make the approach. It will be a good way of finding out if the guards are uninfested humans or human-Controllers.>

When I was fully Andalite, I walked from the narrow alley between Warehouse A and a smaller building.

The two guards posted in front of the warehouse did not look as if they were expecting trouble. One was noisily chewing gum and cleaning his nails with a toothpick. The other was glancing through a newspaper.

I walked forward. <Excuse me. Is this warehouse locked?>

CHAPTER 17

The two soldiers looked up.

One of them gasped and gaped. The gum fell from his mouth.

The second one stepped back. "What in the . . ." But as he studied me, his face lit up with delight. He held out his hand, palm up, as if I were a dog or horse. "I've never seen anything like this." His voice was low and coaxing. "Hey there, fella. Hey!"

<Hay is for horses,> I retorted. <I am not a horse, though in some aspects I closely resemble one.>

I heard Marco roar with laughter. I did not think the situation particularly humorous.

The second guard dropped his gun and

backed up into the first guard. The first guard struggled to keep his balance and reached for his radio.

Now I knew they were not Yeerks.

By now, a Yeerk would have identified me as “Andalite scum” and tried to kill me.

The soldier with the radio pressed a button. But before he could proceed any further, a hairy hand snatched the radio from him. The guard found himself face-to-face with a huge gorilla. He froze.

The second guard dove for his gun. But a large owl swooped down, grabbed the gun in its talons, and flew off.

<We mean you no harm. Now, would you open this warehouse, please?> I asked.

The two guards glanced at each other. The next second they attempted to run. Marco grabbed the first guard and neatly brought him down.

A bobcat jumped gracefully from the roof of the warehouse. It landed on the back of the second guard. The guard fell forward onto his stomach. Tuan stepped calmly from the guard’s back.

<Thanks, dude,> Marco said.

<No problem.>

Tuan slinked away.

With my tail blade I severed the chain that locked the doors of Warehouse A.

Marco and I entered the warehouse.

Marco snorted in disgust.

The warehouse was filled with boxes stacked all the way to the ceiling. On the side of each box was written the word "SPAM" in large black letters.

<What is SPAM?> I asked.

Marco shrugged. <That's what a lot of people would like to know. Come on. This place is just full of provisions. Let's move to the next warehouse.>

We left Warehouse A and carefully approached Warehouse B, our next assignment.

We did not have to speak to the guards. Toby and another Hork-Bajir had captured and restrained them along with the guards from several other warehouses.

It was dark inside the warehouses. But we did not want to turn on the lights for fear of arousing even more suspicion among the conscious Guardsmen on the base. So the adults used flashlights, carefully avoiding shining them near the small windows. Rachel used the owl's night vision to assist the searches. Cassie relied upon the wolf's superior sense of smell to guide her steps.

Our entire retinue was now spread out over the twelve warehouses, hurriedly searching for the munitions that Marco and his father had assured us were stored on the base.

Suddenly I began to feel nervous. There were so many of us. So many different species. So many different levels of experience.

The original Animorphs were used to a small team and tightly controlled missions. Unless the missions got out of control, which they had an unnerving tendency to do.

Still, I was worried. So many things could go wrong. . . .

<Here! Here they are! Warehouse J,> James shouted.

Within moments those members of our larger team not on lookout duty had assembled at Warehouse J.

The munitions were packed in approximately twenty-five, six-foot-long crates. On each crate were printed warnings and admonishments such as "Handle With Care" and "Do Not Open Without Authorization."

<How many crates can we load in two or three trucks and still have room for us?> Cassie asked.

Jake spoke. <I don't know. Probably ten, total? All the new Animorphs will have to travel as birds or fleas on birds. The core group needs to be with the trucks. And the Hork-Bajir will have to squeeze in somehow. It'll be tight. But we have to do this. Come on. Let's load.>

Jake called to Tobias to have the two trucks brought around to Warehouse J.

When the trucks arrived, Toby signaled to two Hork-Bajir. They took up positions on each end of the first crate and grabbed the edges with their large, clawlike hands.

Then they hoisted the crate off the floor.

And a shrieking alarm pierced the night.

CHAPTER 18

<Come on, come on, come on!> Jake called. <I'm demorphing in case I have to talk us out of trouble. Ax, go human. Marco, Rachel, and Cassie, stay in your morphs for now. But hang back. Don't get nasty unless you absolutely have to. James, you guys stay in morph and stay out of sight.>

I began to morph.

Toby's Hork-Bajir stepped up the pace of their loading.

CLUMPclumpclumpclump.

The steady thud of military boots somewhere on base. Twenty, thirty, maybe more National Guardsmen gathering for a showdown.

Shouts.

More alarms.

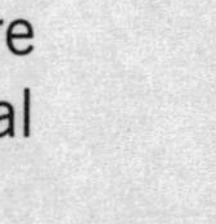

"The Guardsmen are heading for the gates, Prince Jake," I said. "They will attempt to stop and engage us there."

"Hurry! Hurry!" Rachel's mother, from the driver's seat of one of the trucks.

<Yeah, we get it, Mom!> Rachel snapped back.

"Where are you going?" Jake yelled. Marco, still in gorilla morph, stopped and turned to face Jake.

<To get my dad!>

"Stop right now or I'll get Toby to stop you!"

Marco laughed disbelievingly. <You'll do *what*? >

Jake stared stonily. "Get back here. Now!" he ordered.

<I'm going to get my dad,> Marco repeated.

Jake shook his head. "Nobody leaves this fight now. This is it! The real deal. Maybe the last one. We came in together. We're going out together. I'm not risking having to leave one of my team behind. Get it?"

Marco stood, hesitant. Uncertain.

I watched, holding my breath. Jake was Marco's best friend. But it was Marco's father who would be stranded on base, possibly at the mercy of the Yeerks. Would Marco acknowledge Jake's authority? Would this mission hold together?

"For god's sake, Marco," Rachel's mother shouted. "Let's get loaded and get out of here. Your dad will be fine. Come on!"

For once, a bossy and impatient adult was exactly what was needed.

Marco loped back toward the trucks.

At the gate to the base a battalion of soldiers and vehicles was continuing to gather.

We would have to outrun them. And we would have to outrun them with trucks that were loaded with explosives.

The last of the crates had been loaded. We were ready.

"Rachel, Cassie, Marco, demorph!" Jake ordered now. "Get in the trucks. Tobias, stay in the air, okay?"

<You got it, Jake.>

"Good," Jake said. "Remember. We're not going to fight if we can at all help it. We're going to run our butts off."

The Hork-Bajir jumped into the trucks on top of the crates.

Rachel climbed in next to her mother. I squeezed in next to Rachel and slammed the door shut. In the cargo area, Loren and Eva perched precariously.

Marco, Cassie, and Jake jammed themselves into the second truck with Michelle. Cassie's dad took the wheel.

"GO!" Jake shouted.

The small convoy drove slowly but steadily toward the front gate. We did not want to have to knock through a fence. To do so might cause an explosion.

And we had to hope we could get through the open gate without killing innocent National Guardsmen.

But the soldiers were waiting. Of course. Three rows of soldiers. Armed. Rifles at the ready.

Our truck was in the lead. When Rachel's mother saw the barricade of soldiers she automatically slowed down. "What now?" she said. "What now!"

"Ram them," Rachel instructed coldly.

"No!"

"Ram them!" Rachel placed her foot over her mother's on the gas pedal. The truck accelerated.

"Stop it! Rachel! Stop it!" Naomi screamed. "We'll kill them!"

A soldier, obviously a captain, stepped out in front of the troops and held up his hand.

It was a simple gesture. No gun. No threat. Just a request to stop.

Rachel pressed her foot down even harder on her mother's. Naomi yelped.

It was up to me to take control.

"Rachel!" I shouted. "I am ordering you to stop! You must obey my command!"

"Shut up, Ax!" Rachel grabbed the steering wheel with her left hand.

Naomi shoved Rachel toward me, grabbed her daughter's hand on the wheel, desperately tried to regain control of the truck.

But Rachel was too strong. Too determined.

We were going to crash right into the National Guard officer. We were going to kill him.

So I used my strong human arms and grabbed Rachel's hands pulling them from the wheel. It certainly took her by surprise. Her hand slipped from the steering wheel. Her foot from the gas pedal.

With a dreadful screech the truck came to a stop. Not ten feet from the captain.

CHAPTER 19

Rachel turned on me furiously. "What do you think you're doing?"

"Jake gave you an order," I lied.

"What order?" she demanded.

"An order to stop," Naomi said, glancing at me. "I heard it, too."

For a split second Rachel looked stricken. Then the look of fury returned to her face and she slammed her palm on the dashboard.

I turned and looked behind me. The other truck behind us had also been forced to stop.

Jake climbed out of the second truck and walked past us, toward the captain.

The captain, seeing only a boy, visibly relaxed.

This told me that the captain was not a Yeerk. He saw a young human. Not a threat.

If he were a Yeerk he would have a detailed description of Jake and be on the lookout for him.

Jake signaled to the humans to step out of the trucks. They did, and so did I.

"Son! What is going on?" the captain demanded.

"Sir, do you believe in sentient life on other planets?" Jake asked. "Aliens?"

"Is this some kind of a joke?" the captain demanded. "You're in a *lot* of trouble, young man."

"Sir. Please answer the question. I have two trucks loaded with bombs. It's important that you answer my question."

The captain signaled to his men. They began to fan out and surrounded our convoy. Their weapons were held at the ready.

"Son, I don't believe in flying saucers. I don't believe in little green men. And I don't know what this is all about. But I do know that kids and bombs are not a good combination. If this is a school prank, it's a doozy, but . . ."

"Ax," Jake said. "Would you come here, please."

I got out of the truck and walked forward to take my place at his side.

"Sir, did you see the governor on television re-

cently?" Jake asked the captain. "Did you hear her speech about the Yeerk invasion?"

"Of course. But I received word from my major that it was hoax. A very sophisticated hoax. The governor was sent away to a rehab center. Something about drugs or losing her mind. Lieutenant Colonel Larsen is being court-martialed for his association with the governor. Several troops from area bases have been deployed into the city to prevent panic from breaking out."

"Captain, I'm asking you to tell your people not to shoot. You're about to see something disturbing but not dangerous."

The captain considered for a moment before answering. "Okay, son," he said finally. "I'm not sure why I'm giving you my word but I am." The captain turned to his troops and gave the order to hold fire.

"Ax?" Jake said.

I began to demorph.

As I have said, morphing is not pretty and it is not graceful. To the uninitiated it is undoubtedly frightening.

SCHLUUP!

I felt my human face began to tighten. My human lips turned inward and began to seal over.

My human nose receded and was replaced by the distinctive slitted Andalite nose.

CREEEEEEK!

Human shoulders, chest, and arms shrunk and remolded into the narrower, more delicate Andalite shoulders, chest, and arms.

Strong Andalite hindquarters erupted in one smooth motion. My admirable Andalite tail and tail blade followed.

With an audible tinkling sound, my skin was covered with attractive blue-and-tan fur.

Though my eyes were neither fully human nor Andalite, I could see the expression on the captain's face. He looked appalled. I heard him call for a doctor.

"No! No doctors. He's fine," Jake said.

"He's dying," the captain cried hoarsely.

"No, sir, he's not," Jake replied. "He's only demorphing."

CHAPTER 20

I finished demorphing and saw myself surrounded by faces that displayed a range of human emotion. Fascination. Horror. Exaltation. Terror. Even joy.

"They're here!" one soldier cried. "They really are here!"

"Martians?" another guy asked.

"That stuff that's been on the Internet lately. Do you suppose it's true?" a woman whispered.

At that point, Jake gave the signal and the Hork-Bajir came clumping out of the trucks.

The soldiers fell back. I heard clicking and clattering as they shot the bolts of their guns and took aim.

"Remember, sir!" Jake said loudly. "You are not in any danger."

"Hold your fire!" the captain shouted. But his voice shook. He turned to Jake. "I thought it had to be a hoax," he said. "I mean, in a million years . . ."

"Captain, let me explain that just as not all humans are bad, not all aliens are bad, either. The Yeerks are the ones infesting Earth. The Andalites and the Hork-Bajir are our allies."

Jake motioned toward me.

"Captain, may I introduce Aximili-Esgarrouth-Isthill. He's an Andalite. And he's been part of the Earth resistance since the start. His brother, War Prince Elfangor-Sirinial-Shamtul, died fighting to protect Earth from the Yeerks."

The captain nodded. When I held out my hand he hesitated. Then we each stepped forward and shook. Briefly. His hand was much stronger than mine. I resisted the impulse to cringe.

"Toby?" Jake called. With as much grace as a Hork-Bajir can muster, Toby stepped forward from the shadows. Involuntarily, the captain stepped back.

"Toby is the leader of a group of free Hork-Bajir, also valuable members of the resistance. Together we've been fighting the Yeerks. When

we're lucky, freeing more of Toby's people. And maybe someday her home planet."

"It is a pleasure to make your acquaintance," Toby said.

The captain nodded. Murmured something about aliens speaking more perfect English than most of his troops.

"There's one more thing." Jake proceeded to tell the captain the Animorphs' story, beginning with Elfangor. "But now the Yeerks have gotten hold of the morphing techology," he finished. "We've lost our major advantage. It's a bad situation."

The captain's face expressed several contradictory emotions in rapid succession. Disbelief followed by belief. Horror followed by fascination. Finally, he spoke.

"What's the current problem?" he asked.

Jake allowed a small smile to flit across his face. The captain was at least willing to listen further.

"There's a Yeerk pool complex under our town," he explained. "It extends for miles, into every surrounding neighborhood. It's where the Yeerks have to go every three days to feed. There are entrances in every place from fast food restaurants to the mall. It's the largest enemy concentration on the planet. Recently the Yeerks have gotten control of subway trains and six or seven lines of tracks. We figure they did some simple construction that now leads the tracks right into the pool complex. We've seen them herding people at gunpoint down into various subway stations and onto trains. From there, the people are shipped off for infestation." Jake paused and looked intently at the captain. "We need your explosives to blow up the pool complex."

"But I have no orders," the captain protested. "I can't allow you to leave this base with those explosives."

That's when Rachel's mother stepped forward. "Captain Olston!"

"Naomi. What in the world are you doing here?" the captain said.

Rachel's mother and the captain shook hands. "How are you, sir?"

The captain smiled weakly. "Under the circumstances, uh, fine. And still a soldier. Thanks to you."

Rachel's mom turned to the rest of us. "I represented Captain Olston's oldest son when he was wrongfully accused of car theft."

The captain smiled warmly. "You'll never know how grateful my family is. If Robert had been convicted, I probably would have resigned in order to keep pressing his case. You saved my son's future and my career."

He cleared his throat and frowned. “But what’s your role in all of this? Why didn’t you come forward before?”

“I know it sounds insane, Captain Olston, but the Yeerk invasion is real. No matter what you’ve heard about the governor lying or being ill. She was telling the truth and now, obviously, she’s being punished for it.”

“I’m glad to hear the governor’s name cleared,” the captain said. “She’s the best person this state’s ever had in that office.”

“We’re the resistance, Captain,” Naomi went on. “And this . . . this kid,” she said, gesturing toward Jake, “my nephew, Jake, is in charge. So the person to speak to is him. I just thought I’d back him up a little.”

The captain frowned and turned back to Jake. “Son, no offense, but you’re younger than my own youngest boy. He’s a fine young man, but I could never in good conscience send him off to the city with a couple of trucks full of bombs. You don’t actually expect me to allow this, do you?”

Jake spoke firmly but with respect. “We’ll fight our way out of here if we have to, sir. And if we fight, we’ll win. But we don’t want to have to do that. What we really want is your help.”

Suddenly, there was a scuffle and a shout. A shot went wild and barely missed Jake’s head.

Three soldiers wrestled a fourth soldier to the ground.

"Sir," a soldier reported. "Private Grigsby took aim at the boy. He was about to kill him."

Jake turned to the captain. "Grigsby's a human-Controller. That means he's got a Yeerk in his head. There may be more of them in your ranks."

Captain Olston shook his head. "I'm having a hard time taking this all in. As I said, I received orders the other day that the Yeerk invasion story was a huge and elaborate multimedia hoax. I was told that certain troops were needed in the city to prevent panic. The major said that under no circumstances was I to interfere."

"Then your major is a Yeerk," Jake said.

Captain Olston's face turned ashen. "That means . . ."

"It means you have to act on your own authority," Rachel's mother said.

I watched Captain Olston's face and thought I understood his feelings. It is the willingness to take orders from your superiors and then to obey them that keeps an army from becoming a mob.

"Sir," Jake urged. "We don't have a lot of time. There are Yeerks everywhere. We may have been spotted. There may be Yeerks among your own men who have already managed to get word to the city. We must move forward."

Rachel's mother, long Jake's biggest critic,

put her hand on Jake's shoulder. "Listen to him, Captain Olston. He's probably the one who's going to wind up saving our lives. Maybe even the life of the planet."

The captain stared at Jake, and then at me, for what seemed like a long time. Then he cleared his throat.

"What do you need, son?"

CHAPTER 21

Marco's father was summoned from the medical unit to confer. Captain Olston offered men, material, and trucks.

Marco's father first apologized to Captain Olston for having to resort to subterfuge. Then he explained what he considered to be the optimum freight per truck.

"But won't that increase volatility?" Captain Olston asked.

"Yes. But I don't think we have a choice. We're going to have one shot at this. So we want to pack as many explosives onto one train as we can. That means we're going to have to haul a lot of explosives."

"But why not take ten or twenty trucks? We've got them."

"Too many trucks would attract too much attention," Jake said. "Especially if your unit has orders to stay out of the city. But we'll take you up on a few more trucks, if you can spare them. A total of five. And you and some of your people."

We were back at Warehouse J.

The Hork-Bajir and the captain's men had unloaded the explosives and were reloading them so they were packed more stably.

"What about the timers and fuses?" the captain asked.

"I'll set the fuses and the timers," Marco's dad said. "I'm an engineer. Explosives weren't my specialty back before this war but you learn what you have to."

"Please, let my sergeant help you," Captain Olston said. "Explosives are her specialty." He spoke to an assistant who ran off and returned a few minutes later with a small blonde woman. Sergeant Tara Weston.

While she and Marco's father conferred, I hung back and thought.

Though the explosives technology was primitive by Andalite standards, I was fairly confident that it would do the job. If we could get the explosives down into one of the subway stations and onto an empty train.

That was a big "if."

I looked over to where Rachel's mother leaned against the side of her truck, sipping water from a bottle.

I found it interesting that Captain Olston had been grateful to Rachel's mother. Rachel had seemed so sure that her mother was of very little use at all. So had we. But clearly, the captain regarded Naomi the lawyer as very useful.

Because of Rachel's mother, the captain had retained his post. And because he was a smart and honest leader, we were receiving the help we needed.

I began to think Rachel had been unfairly contemptuous of her mother. I think Rachel might have been reaching the same conclusion.

I watched her approach her mother. She did not swagger as she usually did.

Although I do not approve of what humans call eavesdropping, I could not help but overhear some of their conversation.

"Mom," Rachel said softly. "I . . . I'm sorry. I . . ."

"Rachel, it's okay. . . ."

The rest I could not hear. Suddenly, Rachel's shoulders began to shake.

She was crying. It was an odd and disturbing thing to see. But still, I was glad to see her cry.

Rachel is one human for whom I had never

felt pity. But now, I felt an odd sense of kinship. Perhaps Rachel, like me, suddenly realized that the gulf between the present and her childhood was an abyss of loss.

The loading was finished. There were shouted orders as we prepared to depart the base. National Guardsmen and Hork-Bajir scrambled to take their places on five trucks. We planned to morph birds and follow in the air. James and his group had been told to follow us closely.

The parents were thanked and asked to return immediately to camp. There they would wait for news of the mission's success. Or failure.

They did not argue.

Rachel's mother kissed her daughter on the cheek and then stepped back into the shadows.

Marco shook his father's hand and hugged his mother. Proud. But protective.

Tobias had morphed to human to say goodbye to his mother. He held her hand, reassuring her that all would be well.

Cassie and her parents put their arms around each other and touched their foreheads together for a moment before parting.

I knew what was happening. Everyone was saying whatever it is that one says to friends and family when they realize they might be parted forever. I had not had such a chance with either my parents or my brother, Elfangor.

Jake had not had such a chance with his family, either.

Jake, my prince, stood alone and apart.

This might be our last night alive.

I knew he felt keenly the absence of his own family. I could not be his family. He could not be mine. But I could be his friend.

I walked over to him. "You are my prince," I said. "And whatever happens next, know that I am proud to have served you."

Jake smiled wistfully and put his hand on my shoulder. "Ax, for the last time . . ."

"Yes?"

"Don't call me 'prince.'"

CHAPTER 22

We reached the city.

<Okay,> Tobias reported. <There's a subway station on Shawmut Street that's not being used to load people. Yet. But it is under guard.>

<Probably our best bet,> Jake agreed. <Can you get us there?>

Under Tobias's direction, our five-truck convoy rolled through the streets of the city. We Animorphs followed, spread out in the air.

It was early morning, before rush hour. There was little usual commuter traffic. But the sidewalks were packed with people being herded toward subway entrances.

Some wore pajamas and nightgowns and bathrobes.

It was clear that the Yeerk roundup was no longer confined to passersby and motorists. The Yeerks were on the attack. Going from house to house. Rousting people out of their beds and forcing them at gunpoint to the subway stations and then onto the trains.

Our convoy headed up to the Shawmut Street station and pulled to a stop.

Captain Olston jumped out of the first truck and signaled his troops to follow. A small but dedicated and hand-selected group of men and women.

The captain and his troops, guns at the ready, walked briskly toward the small detachment of National Guard soldiers guarding the entrance. The detachment, ten strong, wordlessly closed ranks and put their hands on their weapons.

"Step aside, soldiers," Captain Olston commanded loudly. "We're unloading some equipment."

"Sir," one of the detachment answered. "We have no orders to receive equipment."

"Where is your commanding officer?" the captain boomed.

Immediately, there was the sound of ringing footsteps on metal plated stairs.

The soldiers parted.

A major emerged from the station below and smiled benignly. "Captain Olston! I am surprised

to see you. I believe you had orders to stay on your base."

"I did," Captain Olston said icily. "But those orders have been rescinded."

"On whose authority?" the major asked, his smile looking quite a bit tighter.

"On his." Captain Olston nodded at something behind the major. The major turned and let out a shout of surprise.

Marco, in gorilla morph, took him down.

It all happened too fast for the Yeerk soldiers to react.

A grizzly, a tiger, a wolf, and an Andalite appeared as if from nowhere and quietly knocked the ten men unconscious.

Toby and several Hork-Bajir swarmed from the trucks, gathered the Yeerk major and his soldiers, and hefted them down the subway stairs. In the station they locked the eleven in the toll booth.

Tobias gave the all-clear and assured us he saw no other Yeerk force running to the scene of the ambush. We joined the Hork-Bajir on the subway platform. James and his original team completed our force.

Just as a train came rumbling into the station.

<Here's our train,> Jake said grimly. <Get ready.>

I watched as the first few cars passed before us. Each car was packed with terrified people. Some pressed their faces against the windows. Some pounded and screamed for help. Others just looked stunned and hopeless.

We stood on the platform, waiting to be spotted. And just as we had hoped, the Yeerks commanding the train pulled to an abrupt and screeching stop.

The doors opened. People surged out and pelted for the subway stairs. Those from the first cars, already in the dark tunnel, tore back through the train toward the open platform. All were so terrified, all were so desperate for escape, that they paid no attention to the strange group that stood lined up on the platform.

A grizzly. Rachel.

A gorilla. Marco.

A tiger. Jake.

A wolf. Cassie.

A lion. James.

A crocodile. Collette.

A bobcat. Tuan.

A bull. Kelly.

And an Andalite.

When the train had emptied of uninfested humans, a group of ten human-Controllers in various military uniforms stepped onto the platform.

One of the human-Controllers came forward. "So," he said, laughing, "it looks like the circus is in town." He turned to his companions. "How about we join them in the center ring?"

CHAPTER 23

Immediately, the human-Controllers began to morph.

<Jake!> Rachel's voice was shrill. <Let's get them before they're in battle morphs!>

<No! We give them a fair fight. We fight the Yeerks. We don't become them.>

The first human-Controller morphed to rhino. Another morphed to polar bear. Another to cheetah.

The remaining seven morphed to wolf.

Suddenly, the rhino lowered his head, snorted, and charged!

<Go!> Jake commanded.

Rachel rushed the rhino with the grizzly's surprising speed. They collided!

Rachel's amazing bulk absorbed the majority of the blow, but the rhino's horn caught her in the leg and opened a huge gash.

It was the signal everyone was waiting for.

Battle was joined. Every animal leaped into the fray.

Tuan's bobcat rushed the cheetah. It flipped easily away . . . but Collette was waiting.

SNAAAAAP!

With a crack of the crocodile's deadly jaws, she caught the cheetah's back leg and dragged the cat to the ground. Brutally the crocodile shook the cat from side to side. The cheetah's head slammed against the side of the train. Collette released the still body.

<Marco, behind you!> I warned.

<Got it.>

With a nimble roll, Marco ducked out of the way of the rhino. And gave it a good punch on the head as it passed.

One stalk eye swiveled . . .

FWAP!

One wolf down. But . . .

"Grrrrrrr, grrrrr, grrOWWWWRR!"

Two other snarling, snapping, growling wolves leaped at me. Attempted to back me against the wall.

FWAP!

My tail blade nicked one across the ear.

The bleeding wolf yelped but did not back off. He bared his teeth and snarled more ferociously. The fur along his back bristled. Then, they both jumped at me.

FWAP!

FWAP!

They fell heavily to the platform and lay bleeding. I leaped over their prone bodies. But before I could seek out another opponent . . .

WHUMPF!

Something massive collapsed on top of me! Something huge and smothering.

It was the polar bear.

I struggled to whip my tail, but in vain. The massive weight of the polar bear prevented any part of me from moving at all. I could not breathe. I could not see.

I was blacking out.

Then, I heard rifle shots.

The weight became even heavier. Then suddenly, several Guardsmen were pulling the dead bear off me.

Captain Olston's men had joined us on the platform and opened fire on our attackers. I struggled to my feet. Saw a dead polar bear, a dead rhino, a dead cheetah. And many dead wolves.

Many dead wolves!

My hearts stopped.

I looked in every direction at once.

Where was Cassie?

All about me there was bustle and activity. Our team and Captain Olston's men hurried to unload the trucks waiting outside the station and then to pack the now empty train with bombs.

I galloped from one wolf body to the next. Captain Olston's men would not be able to distinguish one wolf from another.

In the heat of battle, neither would I, unless they were directly attacking me.

Cassie!

I had thought I hated Cassie.

But I did not. I felt for her as I felt for the others. And now she was dead.

I regretted my harsh words. I regretted so much.

"Ax! Come on! We have work to do."

I turned, unable to believe my ears. The voice belonged to Cassie.

She stood beside Jake at the foot of the subway stairs. Both of them had demorphed.

"Come on, Ax," Jake said. "I need you. We've got some decisions to make."

I ran to join them.

I looked at Cassie and she looked at me.

I did not have to tell her that I did not really hate her.

I think she already knew.

CHAPTER 24

The train was packed with explosives set to blow five minutes after the detonator was keyed.

That five minutes would give uninfested humans, human-Controllers, and Hork-Bajir time to run for their lives. I must admit I don't think any of us cared much about the Taxxons' safety.

More than five minutes might give the Yeerks time to figure out how to deactivate the bombs.

"Okay," Jake said. "We're all set. We'll need three people to ride the train. I'll go. That means I need two volunteers to go with me."

"Since this is basically all my fault," Cassie said, "I'm going.

"No way," Rachel argued. "I'm going."

Marco stepped forward. "Jake, I'm sorry, man, but you can't be one of the three."

"Why not?" Jake shrugged. "I'm the only one with no family."

"Maybe. For now," Marco said firmly. "But my point is that the rest of us do have families, right now. Families we care about. You're the one we trust the most. You're the one who's kept us together, kept us alive, and kept us sane. You're the one we trust most to get every one of us out of here and back to camp."

Cassie and Rachel nodded.

<You're the one irreplaceable person in this operation,> Tobias said.

Jake took a deep breath. "Okay. Okay. I'm not saying you guys are right. But we don't have time to argue. You win. But who is going? Remember, whoever goes probably doesn't come back."

I stepped forward. <I will go.>

Jake looked at me for a long time. "Why?"

<For reasons I cannot discuss,> I answered. I was now officially a traitor to my own planet and people. And if the other Animorphs knew that I had been privy to the high command plans of quarantine, they would regard me as a traitor to Earth, as well.

If I did not come back from this mission, perhaps it was best. All I wanted was a chance to die as well as Elfangor. To strike a blow against the Yeerks. To do what I could to bring an end to this war.

Jake asked me no further questions. And I wondered if he knew more than I realized. In a way I hoped so.

Maybe one day, we would have a chance to talk.

One day.

"I'm going," Marco said.

"I'm going," Cassie repeated.

"No way," Rachel argued. "What about me!"

"Cassie's going," Jake said. "If there are tough decisions to be made along the way, I want Cassie to make them. She's as close as I can get to going myself. And Marco's going because . . . I don't know. I guess because he'll enjoy the ride. Rachel, I need you here with me."

Cassie smiled at Jake and he smiled back. Even Rachel looked somewhat appeased.

In spite of the fact that we were all facing almost certain death, somehow it began to feel like old times. Before the war had gotten so terribly ugly.

Somehow, the rifts were beginning to mend. The Animorphs were a team again.

Down the line, we heard the scream of an engine and a whistle.

"Go!" Jake said urgently. "Go. There's another train coming in behind this one. If they see this one stopped, they'll get suspicious."

No one embraced or said good-bye. There was no time. Marco, Cassie, and I ran onto the train and toward the engineer's booth. Marco pressed the lever that powered the train.

The train jerked and began to move forward.

"Come on," Cassie said to me. "Let's do another check. Make sure everything's in place."

The detonators had been set up in the car just behind the engineer's booth. Cassie and I double-checked that everything Marco's father and Sergeant Weston had set in place was indeed in order.

The train picked up speed. We raced deeper into the tunnel. Closer all the time to the Yeerk pool.

The noise of the train's wheels on the tracks grew louder. We rounded a bend.

WHUMPF!

Cassie and I were thrown to the opposite side of the train car.

"We're approaching a station," Marco yelled. "Get down. The Yeerks see an empty train go speeding by, they're going to shoot."

The lights of the station were visible ahead.

Cassie and I ducked. I allowed my stalk eyes

to remain erect so I could glimpse through the bottom sliver of window.

Hork-Bajir and human-Controllers were guarding a large group of people on the platform. They stepped forward, as if expecting the train to stop.

But the train sped through the station.

And the Yeerks began to fire.

CHAPTER 25

Tseeew! Tseeew!

Dracon fire shattered the windows of several cars.

All along the train the lights flickered off, then on again. And I smelled smoke.

Shouting! It was Marco. But I could not understand what he was saying.

The acrid burning smell grew sharper.

I heard the problem before I saw it. A crackling, sizzling, snapping, live cable had detached from the ceiling. It flew madly around the inside of the car like an electrified whip. Blue-and-white sparks shot in every direction.

The cable swung toward us!

Cassie dove under a seat. The cable missed her by inches. "If that thing hits the fuse, it'll blow this train before we get to the pool!" she yelled.

The cable whipped past my head!

I ducked.

"Can't you guys do something?" Marco yelled.

"I'm on it." Cassie rolled out from under the seat, struggled to her feet, and grabbed the overhead passenger bar that ran the length of the car.

<Cassie! No!>

The live cable hit the metal bar! Blue-and-white sparks raced right for Cassie!

Cassie released her grip on the passenger bar a nanosecond before the blue-and-white streak sizzled past her.

The train hurled around a corner. Cassie was thrown roughly to the other side of the car.

So was I. My hooves skidded out from beneath me and I fell heavily on my side.

"Can't we slow down?" Cassie shouted.

"No!" Marco yelled. "I haven't figured out how to work the brake."

Just then, I heard the doors at the back of the car slide open.

And looked up to see a squadron of three Blue Band Hork-Bajir clumping toward us. They

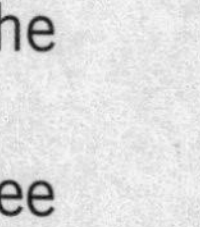

must have been hiding on the train all along. No other explanation. How could we have missed them?

I scrambled to my feet. Tried desperately to keep my balance.

Cassie was not in morph. Neither was Marco.

It was up to me.

I would have to keep the Hork-Bajir from killing us before the train reached its destination.

I readied myself for battle. Curved my tail over my head.

The live cable snapped and sizzled around me.

The Hork-Bajir moved steadily forward, eyes on me, the blades on their knees and elbows whisking.

Then . . .

WHOOOSH!

Something came whizzing through the car door the Hork-Bajir had left open.

A red-tailed hawk!

"Tseeer!"

It buzzed the Blue Bands' heads, raked their heads with its ripping talons!

The train rounded a corner at shocking speed.

And in their startled surprise, the Hork-Bajir reached for the metal passenger bar to steady themselves.

Just as the live cable whipped against it.

ZZZZZAAAAATTT!!!!

The lights in the car flickered off and on. The metal bar turned blue and white. Sparks flew wildly through the air.

I watched the three Blue Band Hork-Bajir turn momentarily translucent as volts of electricity surged through them.

Then, it was over.

The electrical current, overloaded, went dead. And the Hork-Bajir fell to the floor.

Cassie rolled out from beneath the seat.

It was almost pitch-dark. The only light came from the dim lamps set in the tunnel walls.

<Tobias!> I shouted. <Where are you?>

Tobias didn't answer. But I saw the red-tailed hawk dart out a broken window and disappear.

<I do not understand,> I said to Cassie.

But Cassie had run to the window. "Thank you, James," she shouted.

But her voice could barely be heard over the clattering of the racing train.

CHAPTER 26

On and on through the dark tunnel we raced.

The train was now traveling on newly laid track. At intervals we raced past teams of Taxxons and Hork-Bajir, digging at work sites by the light of burning flares.

Some looked curiously at the dark, empty train hurtling past, but then continued with their work.

Marco came out of the engineer's booth. "We're almost there, kids. We're about two minutes from impact. I suggest we start morphing now into survivable forms. Roach or flea. Either one can tolerate all sorts of abuse."

"What about the detonator?" Cassie said.

"I'm going to key it now," Marco said.

"No!" she cried. "You can't key it now. That

only gives the people at the pool three minutes to escape. That's not enough time."

"Cassie!" Marco sighed. "We increase the risk . . ."

<Cassie is right,> I said abruptly. <We agreed to give a full five minutes to those who wish to escape. To give them less would be dishonorable and inhumane.>

Cassie looked at me and smiled.

"Okay. It's two against one. You guys win." Marco paused. "So, who's going to key the detonator?"

"Coin toss," Cassie said quickly.

<What?>

"It's the way we make most major decisions," Marco said dryly. "First, you choose heads or tails. Then you toss a coin. Whatever side is faceup when the coin lands is winner."

The procedure was simple enough. But I could not help but think if this was the methodology by which humans made most of their major decisions . . . Well, it explained much.

<I see. However, a coin has only two sides. And there are three of us.>

"Oh." Cassie. "Right."

"No offense, Cassie," Marco said. "But I think it should be me or Ax."

"Why? You don't trust me to give the people only five minutes to escape?"

"I don't trust you not to sacrifice yourself somehow in the process. No unnecessary heroics. They give me gas."

Cassie looked embarrassed but did not argue further with Marco.

I entered into the decision-making process called the coin toss. I declared "heads" and I "won."

"You know how to key the detonator?" Marco asked, beginning his morph to flea.

<Of course.>

Marco was morphing quickly. <Good luck, Ax-man. See you later.>

I watched as his head shrank to the size of a pin. His arms retracted and disappeared. His body shortened until it was almost flat. And then, zip! He was no larger than a grain of rice.

Dark, scaly material began to cover Cassie's face.

Her arms melted against her sides and wings flared from her shoulders. Her legs shriveled until they appeared to be wires and she fell forward.

In less than thirty seconds, she was a roach. I watched her scurry underneath a seat.

The train zoomed on. We were deep, deep inside the tunnel. All around us was blackness. I poked my head out one of the broken windows and saw the end of the line.

A dim light. The station at the Yeerk pool complex.

One minute had passed.

The train hurtled closer to its destination.

The final station. Where the train was supposed to stop and unload its passengers.

But this train was not going to stop. This train was not going to slow down.

Hork-Bajir and human-Controllers lingered on the station platform. Several watched the speeding train approach with alarm.

The Hork-Bajir and human-Controllers suddenly scattered.

They knew something was wrong.

Thirty seconds.

Twenty-nine seconds.

The detonator. I pressed in the first three digits of the four-digit code. Then I began my morph.

Fortunately, the morph began in my hind end. With any luck, the last thing to go would be a finger.

I am the servant of the people . . .

Fifteen seconds.

I am the servant of my prince . . .

Fourteen seconds.

I felt my tail curl. Experienced an odd, dry, shriveling sensation. My hooves felt papery and

crunchy. My chest cleaved, forming a thorax and belly.

Nine seconds.

Eight seconds.

I am the servant of honor . . .

I could hear shouts and screams now above the clatter of the train. It was clear that a collision was imminent.

Dark, crusty exoskeletal material crept over the backs of my hands. My fingers shortened.

Three seconds.

Two seconds.

I pressed the fourth digit just as my finger disappeared.

The train hit the end of the track and I felt it go airborne.

It arced through the air.

And jackknifed over the Yeerk pool.

CHAPTER 27

The impact was incredible. Even the roach felt it. It was as if the Earth itself had exploded.

I was thrown through the air and hit a surface which could have been anything — a wall, a floor, a ceiling. Thankfully, my lightweight roach body kept me from being injured. Though for a moment or two I felt quite disoriented.

As soon as the motion stabilized, I realized I was floating. The train had landed in the Yeerk pool. The car was filling up with liquid.

I began to demorph. I hoped that Cassie and Marco had also survived.

Fortunately, the car was not completely filled with liquid by the time I had regained my An-

dalite form. My head and shoulders were still above the sludgy water.

Every one of the car's windows had been shattered. Getting out of the wrecked train did not present a problem.

When I emerged it was into a scene of dark and hideous tragedy.

Humans, Hork-Bajir, and Taxxons swarmed toward the crash site.

It occurred to me that the Yeerks had not yet realized that what they had just witnessed was not an accident, but rather, an attack.

Dead slugs were everywhere. Floating on the surface of the pool. Pasted to the sides of the buckled and destroyed train. Scattered all over the docks.

Humans and Hork-Bajir in cages screamed and struggled and begged to be released.

I looked around and saw a familiar head pop up through the gray sludge.

Cassie!

She leaned her head to the side and pounded it with the heel of her hand. Her expression was one of utter disgust. Then I saw her pull a slug from her ear.

She flung it at the side of the train. It made a heavy, wet sound on impact.

"Hey! If you're finished your swim, don't you have an announcement to make?"

Marco! He stood atop the wreckage. He was already morphing.

Cassie climbed up next to him. "Listen to me! Listen!" she cried.

No one paid any attention to her.

"Ax! They can't hear me! Too many of them can't hear me!"

<Keep trying, Cassie!>

She did. And finally people noticed the young girl standing on top of the wrecked train in the midst of the pool. Finally, hundreds of frightened and bewildered creatures listened.

"There are ten one-thousand-pound bombs on this train," Cassie shouted. "They're going to go off in four minutes from now. You have four minutes to evacuate. Anyone still here in four minutes is dead."

If there had been panic before, Cassie's announcement produced utter pandemonium.

Now the Yeerks knew for sure the crash was no accident.

Hork-Bajir stormed for the exits. Knocked over human-Controllers and even Taxxons in their efforts to escape.

Those Controllers with morphing ability began to morph birds, cheetahs, rats. Anything fast. Anything that could fight its way free.

Marco and I raced to the cages where humans and Hork-Bajir were held prior to infestation.

FWAP!

FWAP!

FWAP!

I used my tail to sever bars, locks, chains, and head harnesses. Marco helped the freed people to stand, to take off.

Cassie stood strong in the midst of the streaming mass of creatures. "Get out! Get out!" she yelled. "All of you!"

Several human-Controllers did not run immediately for the exits or the tunnels. Instead, they joined our efforts to free the imprisoned. Perhaps they were unwilling hosts whose Yeerks were currently feeding in the pool. Perhaps they were human-Controllers who worked with their Yeerks as members of the freedom movement.

Quickly these helpers gathered tools and stray pieces of metal wreckage. And began to break open the locks of the cages. Cage by cage they worked to free the prisoners.

I turned back toward the pool. And saw Marco as gorilla struggling with one of the cage. A female human-Controller ran over with a key. She turned it quickly and helped him release the trapped people.

Just as something monstrous rose from the surface of the pool.

CHAPTER 28

The people backed up, and began to run.

I did not wonder at their actions.

The head of the creature in the pool resembled that of an octopus. Twenty bloodshot eyes dotted the bulbous face. Twenty tentacles grew out from the bottom of the head, as large around as eels.

Visser One. Not his most horrifying morph, but certainly bad enough.

<Andalite scum! Vile human resistors! I will tear the heads from your bodies before I let you escape again!>

Marco stood his ground. <You want to fight? We can fight. But it'll be a short fight. About one

and a half minutes. Two minutes, tops. And no winners.>

The visser's bloodshot eyes glared. Slowly he began to move through the thick, viscous layer of dead slugs toward the edge of the pool. Still, Marco stood unmoving. The visser lifted one tentacle, as if to strike Marco. Then swiveled several of his eyes to look once again at the ruined and smoldering train.

<That's right,> Marco said calmly. <Ten one-thousand-pound bombs right behind you. No lie.>

For a moment I thought Visser One would spontaneously combust. Rage emanated from his morphed body. Rage and frustration. He tried to speak but his voice came out as a choked gurgle.

And then the octopuslike creature sank below the surface of the sludgy pool.

No doubt the visser was already morphing to something that would allow him to escape. Visser One always looked after his own interests.

By now the cages were empty of humans and Hork-Bajir alike. The pool complex was largely deserted.

The pool itself remained, stocked with those Yeerks that had not died when the train crashed.

"Time for us to get gone!" Marco ordered.

Rapidly, we morphed to birds. Two ospreys

and a northern harrier. And we took off after the escaping horde.

Wings working madly we raced along one of the tunnels through which crowds of escaping Hork-Bajir, Taxxons, human-Controllers, and uninfested humans were frantically scrambling their way to the surface. To freedom.

Birds of every kind screeched and smashed into walls in their panic to get out. People were knocked on the floor, stepped on by humans too panicked to think.

All around us was chaos and madness and fear. It was the saddest thing I had ever seen in this horrible war. Desperation brought on by the knowledge of imminent death.

We had just cleared the first major loop up and away from the pool complex when the first bomb exploded.

BA-BOOOOOM!

There was a short delay and then it was as if a hurricane fueled by a blast furnace had come raging through the tunnel.

Large areas of the roof fell in. The floor buckled and collapsed. My ears were bombarded by screams and cries and shrieks.

I had lost track of Cassie and Marco. I did not know what to do except keep flying. The air was almost solid with dust and debris. The heat was overwhelming. But still I flew.

BABOOOOM! BABOOOOM! BABOOOOM!

Explosions reverberated through one cavernous tunnel after the other.

Finally, miraculously, where the ceiling had caved in up ahead, I saw light. Just a pinpoint. But it was enough.

I flew toward it, rising out of the hideous underground into the open sky.

CHAPTER 29

Late that day, we perched on the roof of one of the few skyscrapers left in the area.

The destruction was breathtaking. Below us, there was a sinkhole where much of downtown had been.

Everything had just caved in. Half the mall, several office buildings, train stations, stores — all were gone.

Most of downtown had simply collapsed, swallowed up by an explosion the size of a small nuclear blast.

The buildings still standing were cracked. Some listed to the side.

The entire area was ringed with fire engines, ambulances, military vehicles, and onlookers.

<Well,> Marco said thickly, <we did some serious damage. Just like we hoped to do. I'll bet we killed a million Yeerks.>

<Yeah,> Cassie agreed, no note of satisfaction or joy in her voice.

I felt no sense of satisfaction or joy, either. There were many bodies down there. Human bodies. Taxxon bodies. Hork-Bajir bodies.

And perhaps three of the dead or mortally wounded were Jake's parents and brother. I knew we were all wondering if they had been at the pool when the explosion occurred. I also knew none of us would talk about it. Not to Jake and not to each other.

What could we possibly say?

Also, I could not forget that many human-Controllers had lingered in order to save other humans who were not Controllers.

I suppose I had always known that Cassie was right. Always known but had been reluctant to admit that Aftran had not been the sole member of a Yeerk resistance movement. That there were many Yeerks who, given a choice, would choose not to conquer. Would choose not to kill. If they ever were lucky enough to be given such a choice.

Yes. Cassie was right.

We heard the heavy flap of wings and Jake in peregrine falcon morph settled beside us.

<Everybody's back at camp and safe,> Jake

said. <Captain Olston and his troops got out of the area in time.> Jake paused. Then said, <Good job.>

<I don't know,> Rachel said slowly. <There's no telling how many human-Controllers the Yeerks created down there in the past week. Thousands maybe. No telling how many escaped.>

<Yes,> Jake agreed. <But without the pool, the Yeerks have no way to feed. It'll be a pretty horrible three days, but at the end, we're going to have a lot more dead Yeerks. And a lot of humans who have no illusions about what we're fighting against. Not to mention the Hork-Bajir who'll be freed, too.>

<Well, that's something,> Marco pointed out. <But you know what the saddest thing about this whole situation is?>

<I wouldn't even know where to begin,> Cassie answered.

<The saddest thing is that this is our greatest victory. And I've never felt more depressed in my entire life.>

<Well, just when you think you can't get any more depressed,> Tobias said, <look who's dropping in.>

A large gray shadow fell over the city. We looked up and saw Visser One's Blade ship hovering, a swarm of Bug fighters surrounding it.

<I guess it was too much to hope that he wouldn't survive,> Marco said gloomily.

<No telling what kind of morph got him through,> Tobias commented. <But we've hurt him. And he'll have some explaining to do to the Yeerk High Council.>

<Come on,> Jake directed. <We're of no use here anymore. Let's get back to camp.>

One by one we took off and winged our way back home.

Visser One wasn't the only one who would have some explaining to do.

I, too, would have to justify my actions to an angry Andalite high command. If I chose ever to speak to the Andalites again.

They would never understand and I would never be able to explain.

But for good or ill, I had thrown in my lot with the humans.

Humans.

Violent but peace-loving.

Passionate but cerebral.

Humane but cruel.

Impulsive but calculating.

Generous but selfish.

Humans. Altogether a contradictory and deeply flawed species.

And yet . . . And yet, somehow I knew that they represented the best hope of the galaxy.

Perhaps the only hope.

<Ax.> Jake, addressing me in private thought-speak.

<Yes?>

<Thank you,> he said.

<You are welcome,> I answered. Then to myself, I mentally added, <Prince Jake.>

Don't miss

ANIMORPHS®

#53 The Answer

"It's too dangerous." That was Eva, Marco's mom. The woman who had been host body to the first Visser One. "Visser One will know that you know. He'll know you're coming. He can't let you destroy a pool ship — that's the only large-scale food supply the Yeerks have. The Blade Ship can only service so many. Lose a pool ship? The Council of Thirteen would have Visser One executed."

Marco shook his head. "He'll think we're cocky after taking out the Yeerk pool. Maybe he'll underestimate us."

"No," Eva said flatly. "He'll never underestimate you again. That's over."

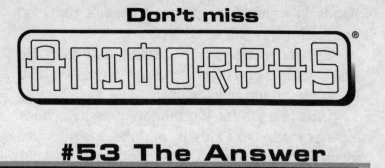

We stood around a small fire. It was chilly. Fog had a tendency to form in this deep valley, sometimes so thick we could barely see our hands in front of our faces. It wasn't that bad now, but it was still cold.

"It's too dangerous," Cassie's dad said. He was sipping a cup of what passed for coffee here in our rough-and-ready camp.

"This is a job for the military now," Rachel's mom argued. "You kids have done enough. The secret is out: Leave it to the people who should be protecting this country. I mean, we paid enough in taxes to support the military, well, now let's see what we got for all that money."

We were in a council of war. I was getting so I hated these meetings. Too many voices, too many opinions. So many opinions sometimes that it seemed the consensus would always come down on the side of doing nothing.

But we were guests among the free Hork-Bajir. This was their valley, their trees, the only home they had. We'd come running to them with our families in tow when we needed a place to hide. So at very least I had to listen to Toby, the young female Hork-Bajir seer. And only a fool would dismiss Eva's input: None of us knew the Yeerks half as well. And of course, there were my fellow Animorphs.

But added to all that we had Marco's dad; Rachel's mom; James, the representative of our new, adjunct Animorphs; Tobias's mom; both of Cassie's parents, who only cared about making sure no one got hurt . . . too many people with too many agendas. But I still didn't know how to tell adults, my friend's parents no less, to be quiet and let me do my job.

I tried not to show my impatience, but these days I'm not so good at that. Cassie was watching me. We're not as close anymore, but she still knows me.

She said, "Look folks, we're going to try. I don't think the question is really 'whether' but 'how.'"

"No one has decided any such thing," Rachel's mom said angrily. "My daughter is not going to be dragged into some suicidal undertaking like this."

Rachel laughed. Rachel's not a person who'll be one way with her friends and another way with her family. There's only one version of Rachel. "Mom, if we go, I go. If we don't go, I still go. Visser One parks his pool ship right out in the open and we're not going to ram it down his nonexistent throat? Hah! I'm with Marco: Blow it up. Blow it up real good."

I hid a grin. Rachel is the original Nike girl: Just do it. Just do it, and if that doesn't work do it harder and meaner.

"It seems a waste to simply blow it up," Toby said, speaking for the first time. The Hork-Bajir are a fearsome-looking, but basically peaceful race that, left alone, would live in the trees eating bark and caring for the forest. Toby is one of a rare Hork-Bajir mutation: a seer. A sort of Hork-Bajir intellectual and leader. She leads the free Hork-Bajir, a small but growing band of Hork-Bajir who have been liberated from their parasitic masters.

"What do you mean?" I asked Toby.

"There are hundreds of captive Hork-Bajir aboard the Pool Ship," Toby said. "If we could free at least a portion of them . . . and of course there are the ship's massive weapons systems. Imagine controlling all that power."

"Take it?" Marco yelped. "*Steel* the Pool Ship!"

Rachel jabbed a finger at Toby. "This is my girl," she said.

Rachel's "girl" was nearly six and a half feet tall, and looked an awful lot like a kid's notion of a goblin. Not to mention the fact that she was armed with razor-sharp blades growing from wrists and elbows and forehead.

<It's the approach Visser One would not expect,> Ax opined cautiously. <It is of course impossible. It's not like stealing a Bug Fighter. Every system on-board the Pool Ship is encrypted, and the codes will probably change hourly. It might take me an hour to break any one sequence, and if I'm a minute late it will roll over

and I'll be starting back at the beginning. An hour to get you into navigation, for example, if I'm lucky. And another hour to gain access to weapons systems.>

And then everyone started talking at once, arguing, posturing, scoring debating points.

"Okay," I said, holding up my hands for calm. "That's enough, folks, thanks for coming."

"You don't just dismiss us!" Rachel's mom yelled.

"Sure he does, Mom," Rachel said cheerfully.

"I need Rachel, Marco, Tobias, Ax, Toby, James, and Eva," I said.

I hadn't meant to exclude Cassie. I really hadn't. But it was too late. She looked like I'd hit her. She blinked and turned quickly away, covering the moment with aimless chatter to her parents.

Tobias gave me a dirty look. And if you think a red-tailed hawk's gaze is always a dirty look, you're close to being right. Still, I knew Tobias was mad at me. Everyone was. Everyone but James who was excited to be included, and Eva who hadn't really caught what was going on with me and Cassie.

There was nothing to be done now. I couldn't go running after Cassie. The insult had been delivered. There was no taking it back now.

I said, "As much as I hate to admit it,

Rachel's mom is partly right: This isn't just our fight anymore. Three pilots died today. Probably Air National Guard. It shows that there are military forces out there that could help."

"All due respect," Marco said, "those pilots didn't do much good."

"If we're going after the pool ship we need a diversion," I said. "We'll need a great, big diversion. I want tanks and jets and soldiers. And I want us — some of us at least — to be right out there in front with them. I want Visser One to be dead sure we're trying to either blow up his precious ship or get inside it."

"And we will be, right?" James asked. "I mean, one or the other, right?"

I shook my head. "Visser One will consider the possibility that we're using the attack as a cover. He's slow but he's not a complete idiot. He'll figure one of three things: First, the attack is the real thing. Second, the attack is a cover for a second attack. Third, the attack is a cover for us to infiltrate the ship and destroy it from inside. Any of those three options he does the same thing: lifts the ship off and amuses himself blasting everything in sight with the pool ship's big Dracon cannon."

"Okay," Toby said. "I give up: How is he going to be wrong?"

"When the diversion comes, we'll already be

on board the pool ship, working on breaking those access codes," I said. "The diversion won't be to cover us getting on. It'll be to cover the fact that we're already there."

It sounded good. Sounded like I had a plan.

I didn't.

I pulled Tobias and Marco aside after the Council of War.

"Tobias? Did you notice that pillar of smoke off to the south of where we were?"

Tobias glared at me. <What you did to Cassie was beyond wrong.>

I squirmed. "I don't have time for that, Tobias."

<Cassie is one of us,> he said.

"Did you see the smoke or not?!" I demanded.

<Yeah.>

"Then I need you to go find out exactly where it's coming from. Now. I mean, if you can spare the time from busting me."

Tobias didn't answer. He just spread his wings and flapped till he cleared the trees and then caught a tail wind out of sight.

Marco gave me a fish-eyed look, but he didn't say anything.

"Marco, we need to know who is currently in charge of military forces in this area."

Marco thought that over. "It's not going to be

just one guy. You'll have an Air Force general, a Marine, an Army guy."

I nodded. "Yeah. But the Pentagon will have given someone the weight, you know? Someone is going to be in overall command. I mean, if they haven't done that at least . . . They can't be that sorry, can they? I want you to get me a name and a location. Grab Ax. Use him to creep Pentagon computers or whatever it takes. I need the person who can give orders and have them followed in this area."

"How about the Chee? They'd be able to help us out."

I shrugged. "Where are the Chee? That's the problem. Those Bug fighters smoked the King house. I don't think it would have damaged their underground complex, but with the house gone how do we make contact?"

"Guess that's two problems for me and Ax," Marco said.

"Yeah." I hung my head. "I didn't mean to do that with Cassie. It was . . . stuff happens sometimes."

"Uh-huh. I better get going."

In twenty-four hours I had two of the three answers I was looking for. Marco did not find the Chee. He did find what he hoped and believed was the man in charge of military forces arrayed against the Yeerks.

"He's an Army general. Three star. His name is Sam Doubleday. He's fifty-four years old. His headquarters is fifty miles from here, though. In the hills, some kind of nuclear shelter in a hollowed-out mountain."

"Good. At least he's not dumb enough to be right here where the Yeerks can't help but kill him."

The second piece of information was more intriguing.

<They're building a new Yeerk pool,> Tobias reported. <Not so much a cave like the old one. More like they're digging a small lake and going to let it be open. Taxxons are all over the place, like maggots on a piece of roadkill.>

I could see that Marco was preparing some witty remark on the fact that Tobias was unusually familiar with roadkill. I shot him a look and he sighed, letting it go.

A second Yeerk pool being built at frantic pace. That made sense. Once it was finished the Yeerks would remove the pool ship back to safety in orbit. Taxxons were natural tunnelers, faster and more effective than anything Caterpillar made. It was like having a few hundred giant sentient earthworms at work.

"Okay," I said. "Let's go see this general."

<Who goes?> Tobias asked pointedly.

"Animorphs," I said. But of course I knew what he was asking. "All of us. I'll have James's people come in to watch the camp here. The rest of us, the six of us, we go to see the general. Wait, ask James to come, too. He can use the experience."

<Well, you'll need to go ask Cassie yourself,> Tobias said primly.

"Marco: Let everyone know. *Everyone.*" I avoided looking at Tobias. Not often do I feel like a coward, but I felt like one right then. . . .